Maggie looked so very...kissable.

A laugh from the bunkhouse brought him back to reality. What was he thinking? She was a participant in his program.

"Um...good night, Joe."

"Night, Maggie." He headed down the path, then stopped. "The phone number to the bunkhouse is right by the phone. Call if you need anything—anything at all."

He gritted his teeth. That sounded like a proposition, and he hadn't meant that at all.

"I mean...uh..." He couldn't think.

"I know what you mean, Joe. See you bright and early in the morning."

He caught himself whistling as he walked to the bunkhouse. He hadn't whistled in ages.

But sleep wouldn't come. He kept thinking about Maggie, who had a wagonload of trouble she had to deal with. Her heaviest cargo was the smallest kid in Cowboy Quest.

Would he be able to help her?

Dear Reader,

The Cowboy Code kicks off my new miniseries, Gold Buckle Cowboys, which I hope you'll love reading as much as I've enjoyed writing. The gold buckle symbolizes the cowboy's victory over wild bulls, broncs or steers in competition. Every cowboy wants a gold buckle—even more than money. The buckle is a conversation piece, a good pickup topic for a "buckle bunny," and it can be pawned when a cowboy is down and out—although he'd rather cut off an arm!

My Gold Buckle Cowboys are honorable men with hearts of gold and a trophy case full of gold buckles. They are cowboys who turn to mush over kids and can be tamed only by women who are as strong as they are.

They are cowboys who will win your heart in eight seconds!

What woman wouldn't want a Gold Buckle Cowboy's boots under her bed?

I'd love to hear from you! I can be contacted at www.christinewenger.com or at P.O. Box 2000, Cicero, NY 13039.

Cowboy up!

Chris Wenger

THE COWBOY CODE

CHRISTINE WENGER

Silhouette

SPECIAL EDITION

Published by Silhouette Books
America's Publisher of Contemporary Romance

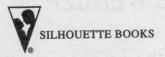

SILHOUETTE BOOKS

ISBN-13: 978-0-373-65576-2

Recycling programs
for this product may
not exist in your area.

THE COWBOY CODE

Visit Silhouette Books at www.eHarlequin.com

Printed in U.S.A.

CHRISTINE WENGER

has worked in the criminal justice field for more years than she cares to remember. She has a master's degree in probation and parole studies and sociology from Fordham University, but the knowledge gained from such studies certainly has not prepared her for what she loves to do most—write romance! A native central New Yorker, she enjoys watching professional bull riding and rodeo with her favorite cowboy, her husband, Jim.

Chris would love to hear from readers. She can be reached by mail at P.O. Box 2000, Cicero, NY, 13039 or through her website at christinewenger.com.

To my wonderful sister-in-law, Jean Matyjasik,
for her friendship, laughter and good nature.
And she can make a really good babka!

Chapter One

Maggie McIntyre couldn't wait to unfold herself from the dusty wreck of a pickup truck sent from the Silver River Ranch.

It had been a long, tedious day that had started at dawn, when her nephew Danny was released to her from juvenile detention in lower Manhattan. Then they had had to change planes three times—starting at JFK International Airport—before they'd finally landed at this blip on the map called Mountain Springs, Wyoming.

And throughout the day, Danny had barely spoke three words to her, civil or otherwise.

To alleviate his worries—if he was indeed

worrying—she'd tried to convince him that the Cowboy Quest Program would be a good experience for both of them, but she had a feeling that her monologue had fallen on deaf ears.

Still, Maggie hoped that at least some of her words would sink in. Maybe Danny would realize that they were in Cowboy Quest together—as a family—and not only would they work on their communication skills and strengthen their bond, but they'd have a good time, too.

Where else could they learn to rope, ride horses, go on a cattle drive and basically live differently than what they were used to? It would be an experience that they'd remember their entire lives.

As she spoke, Danny remained silent and aloof.

Would there ever come a day when she'd be able to reach him? What had happened to the sweet boy that she'd watched grow up? When had he turned into a hostile and shuttered thirteen-year-old?

Finally, after a long, bumpy drive, they pulled into the entrance of the ranch. As far as she could see in the dusky light, there were miles of emerald-green grass shimmering in the spring breeze.

So this was the Wild West—although she hoped it wasn't *too* wild.

Maggie paused a moment before opening the door and studied the ranch house in front of her. Floor-to-ceiling windows jutted out from the middle of the two angled wings, and it reminded her of a bird—in this case, an eagle—about to take flight.

The house—if that was the right term—sat regally on a hill overlooking several outbuildings and the surrounding countryside. Brick walkways led to some of these outbuildings.

Maggie couldn't wait to explore.

Their driver, Quint, who was as quiet as Danny during the drive here, opened the door of the truck for her, and Maggie stepped onto a soft patch of Wyoming grass.

"C'mon, Danny," she said, zipping up her designer fleece coat. "We're here."

No answer.

"Aren't you going to get out of the truck, son?" Quint asked.

In response, the wizened cowboy got a bored shrug from the sullen teenager.

Maggie hoped that the change of scenery would be what she and Danny needed to rebuild and strengthen their relationship, but that wouldn't happen if he wouldn't even get out of the truck.

Maggie had only herself to blame for the chasm between Danny and herself. When her sister, Liz, died two years ago—four years after the boy's father—leaving her as Danny's sole guardian, Maggie had immersed herself even more in her acting, her escape from the painful loss of the sister she'd so loved. Besides, she was a single mother now, and she needed to support herself and Danny. With a heavy heart, she'd realized too late that her absence from Danny had done him more harm than good. At a time when he'd needed her the most, she'd been working long hours—and Danny had been getting into trouble.

She had to have faith that Joe Watley's Cowboy Quest program would be her nephew's salvation—and hers, too.

She hoped that Cowboy Quest would somehow help Danny realize that their shared grief was keeping them apart, and that he was acting out because he was afraid of losing her, too. Her job would be to help Danny accept the fact that he'd never lose her. She'd always be in his life, always be there for him.

If she and Danny were able to accomplish these important things, they would be well on their way to becoming a real family, and Maggie wanted that more than anything.

If Danny successfully completed the program, the family court wouldn't place him in a juvenile correctional facility.

If Danny were placed, that would mean she had failed him, and Maggie couldn't stand to bear that burden. Liz had given up so much to help Maggie's career in the theater. If she failed Danny, it would be like failing Liz, too.

As she looked around, she noticed a man walking

toward her—a big hulk of a man. Judging by his white hat and saucer-sized belt buckle, she concluded that he was definitely a cowboy.

Maggie tried not to stare at him, but she couldn't help herself. She felt as if she was being pulled toward him by some unknown force. He was the epitome of what she thought a real cowboy would look like. His straight black hair was pulled into a ponytail with a string of rawhide, and he wore a long-sleeved chambray shirt tucked into a pair of faded denim jeans.

If his high cheekbones were any indication, he might even have some Native American blood. His skin was a deep shade of brown, but that could be just from all the outdoor work he must do.

There weren't many cowboys in Manhattan, but he'd certainly stand out in a crowd among any. He'd probably stand out in a crowd here in Wyoming, too.

But what credentials did this big cowboy have, other than the fact that the family court judge seemed to have absolute faith in him? Could she really trust him with her nephew?

And why wasn't there any information about the program online?

He stopped in front of her and smiled warmly. "Welcome to the Silver River Ranch. You must be Maggie McIntyre." He yanked a brown leather work glove off and held out his hand. "I'm Joe Watley, and I'm in charge of the Cowboy Quest program. Sorry I wasn't able to pick you and Danny up at the airport myself, but there was a problem with one of my bulls."

Maggie held out her hand, and as he engulfed it in his, she felt a shock zip through her body, and all her senses were suddenly on alert. His calloused grip told her that he did more than run a program for juvenile delinquents and oversee a ranch. He did hard work.

He released her hand and tugged his glove back on. "The vet had just arrived, so I couldn't leave, but I'm sure that Quint took good care of you."

"He did. And Mr. Watley, I'd like to thank you for accepting my nephew into your program," she said with more conviction than she actually felt.

"Call me Joe." He pushed his hat back with a thumb. "I believe that you're participating in my program, too, Ms. McIntyre."

Judge Cunningham felt that six weeks of Joe's Cowboy Quest program would be a good bonding experience for *both* of them—in fact, he'd made it a condition of her ability to maintain custody. Maggie hoped with all her heart that this program would solve all their problems.

"It's good to be here." Maggie forced herself to keep her eyes on Joe's and stop her inspection of his muscular body. "Danny is very happy to be part of your program and be here on your ranch."

"I doubt that very much, since he won't even get out of the truck." Joe's onyx eyes twinkled and a smile twitched at the corner of his mouth. "And I doubt that you're thrilled to be here, either. It's a far cry from Broadway."

"You know about me?" Maggie asked.

"I have a copy of the probation officer's report."

"I see," she said, unnerved. "Well, I'm here for Danny, and I'm going to do my best."

"So will I."

Maggie remembered the serious probation officer who'd come to her SoHo apartment to interview her and Danny in order to prepare an investigation. The officer had stated that the report would go to the judge to assist him in deciding what to do with Danny. Now Joe had a copy of the report. Maggie didn't know if she wanted him or his staff or anyone else knowing about her family problems, but then again, he probably needed the information in order to help.

Still, what could this cowboy do, when the best social workers and psychologists in New York City couldn't get Danny to change his behavior?

Maggie looked back at the pickup. Danny still sat in the front seat, and Quint still stood by the opened passenger door, looking amused. The set of the boy's shoulders told Maggie exactly what Danny was thinking—he wanted to be anywhere but here.

But they were both here because Danny had been acting as a lookout while his so-called friends were burglarizing a nearby grocery store. The others had gotten away, but Danny was arrested and refused to name the others involved.

She'd had a talk with him about being a leader instead of a follower, but apparently it hadn't sunk in, judging by his attitude.

She met Joe's gaze and stiffened her shoulders. This would be just as hard as she'd thought.

Maggie began walking toward the pickup to have a word with Danny, but Joe placed his hand on her shoulder. "I'll take care of it. He's my responsibility now."

His light touch was warm and reassuring, and Maggie felt the same relief wash over her as she felt when the curtain closed at the end of a performance and the audience erupted in applause. It was then, and only then, that she could relax.

But she couldn't relax here. The Cowboy Quest program would be work, *hard* work. Her plan was to throw herself into the program just like she did when she prepared for a new role. She loved Danny as if she'd actually given birth to him, and she would do whatever it took to heal their broken relationship.

Joe walked over to where Danny sat. "Welcome to the Silver River Ranch, partner. I'm Joe Watley. I'm in charge of the program."

Maggie let the low timbre of his voice wash over

her, relax her. Joe didn't waste a word, and he spoke with complete confidence and authority.

Danny looked away, but Joe pressed on. "I hope you don't expect Quint to unload your luggage. Every cowboy here hauls his own weight, and that means you, too. We'll get you settled in the bunkhouse, and then we'll take your aunt's things to the main house."

"The main house?" Danny asked, looking up for the first time.

"Did you expect her to stay in the bunkhouse with the other participants?" Joe asked with a grin.

"Where are you going to be?" Danny asked. Sarcasm dripped from his voice like icicles melting from a roof.

"I'll be staying in the bunkhouse with everyone else." Joe met Danny's eyes. "And it's to your credit that you're looking after your aunt. Being respectful to women is part of the Cowboy Code."

"The Cowboy Code? Spare me." He rolled his eyes. "That's lame."

"It's not lame. The Cowboy Code consists of general rules for gentlemanly behavior—things that any good citizen should follow. And believe it or not, you got one of the components." Joe grinned. "One down, several to go."

Danny didn't turn away, but blinked, stunned. Slowly—grudgingly—he climbed out of the truck.

Maggie was impressed with Joe's response to Danny's sarcasm. He'd taken what could have been a sensitive subject and ended it on an upbeat note.

Was Danny worried that she and Joe might get close?

She wondered, not for the first time, what went on in a thirteen-year-old boy's head. Why would he think that they'd live under the same roof and get involved just like that? Merciful heavens, she'd just met the man.

Was Danny worried that she'd spend more time with Joe than with him?

Then it dawned on her. Steve Rayborn. She remembered when Danny had thought that she was serious about Steve, a costar in her last musical. A dear friend, he'd helped her through Liz's two-year battle with cancer and her ongoing struggle to act like a parent. When Maggie finally confronted Danny about his silent treatment and rude remarks toward Steve, the boy had admitted that he thought Maggie was going to marry Steve and that they wouldn't want him.

Realizing how frightened her nephew was of losing the only family he had left, Maggie explained that Steve was just a friend, and that Danny would always be first and foremost in her life.

Now, though, it seemed that Danny's old insecurities were resurfacing. But she hoped that Cowboy Quest would finally put her fears to rest. Sure, Joe was out of the ordinary and handsome enough to be a leading man, but Maggie had enough to deal with right now without adding romance to her life. Besides, she was too worried about Danny's future to think about starting something with Joe, or anyone else for that matter.

She'd have to try and explain that to her nephew and encourage him to take this program more seriously. He didn't seem to care that he could be placed in foster care.

As she watched Joe and Danny hauling luggage together, she looked up at the vibrant colors of the setting sun and said a little prayer that Joe would be able to reach the boy.

Joe motioned for her to join them. "Maggie, come and see the bunkhouse. It's not much, but Danny's going to call it home for six weeks."

They walked in silence with nothing but the crunch of the gravelly path under their feet. In front of them stood a long stretch of clapboard building with several windows and an inviting porch with a dozen white rocking chairs. Some swayed slightly in the late-spring breeze, as if ghostly inhabitants were enjoying an evening break.

Joe knocked on the door. "Lady present. Is everyone decent?"

She could hear the scraping of chairs and the sound of boots on a wooden floor.

"Yeah, boss. C'mon in." The voice sounded like Quint's.

As Joe opened the door, seven cowboys stood at attention, holding their hats in their hands.

Joe introduced them. "Adriano, he's my foreman. This handsome gent is Guillerme, or Willy for short. And this tall son-of-a-gun is Ronnie. Gentlemen, I'd like you to meet Dan Turner and his aunt, Maggie McIntyre."

There were four more cowboys present whose names she promptly forgot. She forced a smile and shook hands, wondering again how these men could possibly help Danny.

What on earth was Judge Cunningham thinking?

Danny halfheartedly shook hands with them all, but he wasn't smiling. Right now he seemed younger than his thirteen years. His long, narrow face sprinkled with freckles made him look about ten years old. He was thin, bordering on skinny, but his fierce blue eyes were the windows to his soul. And right now, his soul wasn't happy.

Maggie gave the bunkhouse a quick glance. The walls were just plywood, and there was nothing to give the big room color other than a calendar with a green tractor urging insurance in case of ranch accidents.

A long, beat-up table sported coffee-ring stains, an array of assorted mugs and lots of dig marks, no doubt made by the men's spurs when they put their feet up on the table.

A fairly new galley kitchen ran half the length of the room, but what she noticed the most was the monstrous coffeemaker on a round table by the stove. In fact, the whole place smelled of coffee.

"Danny, you're the first participant to arrive. The others will be here any time now," Ronnie stated. "You get to pick your bunk."

"I don't care," Danny said, but Maggie noticed that he looked around and drifted toward one of the metal cots by a window.

He's probably planning his escape route, she thought.

The bunkhouse was certainly a few stories down from their apartment in SoHo. And here Danny didn't have his own bedroom.

Joe held out his hand to shake Danny's. "I'll see you later for grub. Make up your bunk and get settled in, and I'll escort your aunt to the main house. When the others arrive, the boys will show you all around the ranch."

Danny shook Joe's hand but didn't meet his gaze, looking at the floor. Maggie tried to swallow the lump in her throat, saddened that Danny would freeze out the man who was his best shot at a fresh start.

She willed herself to believe that coming here had been a good idea.

As she followed Joe up the hill to the house, Maggie noticed that the rambling stone and log structure somehow fit perfectly into the landscape. A snow-capped mountain range and a copse of conifers peeked over the roof, completing the picture.

Maggie stared in awe. "What a breathtaking house. I can't wait to see inside."

There was still a fairly steep climb on a land-scaped brick walkway to get to the front door.

Joe smiled. "My father built it for my mother when they were first married. She's Lakota Sioux, and he constructed the house with twelve beams, just like the Lakota teepee was constructed with twelve poles. And the door faces east, which repre-sents the rising sun and a new day."

She'd been right. He *was* part Native American.

She stole a glance at Joe. Effortlessly carrying her heavy suitcase and tote bag, he wasn't even breath-ing hard. Every arm muscle bulged under his shirt. His thighs looked rock-hard under his jeans.

His physical appearance made her heart pump faster, but there was so much more to Joe. He seemed to have a quiet dignity and an almost inner peace about him, as if he knew the secret of keep-ing centered. She hoped he'd share his secret with Danny, and her, too.

Maybe Danny was right to worry. She *was* inter-ested in Joe.

But she wasn't interested in him in a romantic

way. He intrigued her, probably because he was just so different from the men she knew. That didn't mean that they were going to start something, like Danny seemed to think.

Not when her main concern was her nephew and getting him through Cowboy Quest.

She might as well add herself to that. She had to get through Cowboy Quest, too, and she didn't know the first thing about riding a horse or going on a cattle drive.

But one thing she did know was that she was going to do her best and then maybe, just maybe, she and Danny would become a closer, happier and stronger family.

Chapter Two

Joe felt the burn in his muscles from carrying Maggie's suitcases up the hill to his house.

Good. It took his mind off her—a little.

She was a strikingly beautiful woman. Her hair shimmered like spun gold in the afternoon sun, and her green eyes were bright and sparkly. Even if he hadn't already known from reading the probation department's report, he could tell she was a dancer by the way she moved—graceful and light on her feet. She almost floated when she walked.

She didn't seem to be the type who could handle mucking out stalls, grooming horses or several days on a cattle drive.

He opened the door to let her in. "Make yourself at home. My Aunt Betty is usually here in the office doing the record keeping and running my life, not necessarily in that order, but she's visiting her sister in Tucson for a couple of months. So the place is all yours."

"I can't imagine having this whole house to myself. This is magnificent, Joe. My apartment in New York can fit into it about forty times!" Her excitement faded. "But if I wasn't here, you could have stayed in your home instead of at the bunkhouse."

"No, I always bunk with the kids during Cowboy Quest. So make yourself at home."

The only other woman who had ever stayed at his ranch was Ellen Rogers. Ellen had stolen his heart when she kissed him on the playground in fourth grade, after he'd stopped some boys from teasing her.

That was about the time he learned that he didn't have to start swinging his fists to get his point across. His size alone—even in grade school—made him seem formidable.

They'd become lifelong friends after that. Inseparable. Her parents had the neighboring ranch, about twenty miles away, and their spread was almost as big as the Silver River.

He'd asked Ellen to marry him when they graduated from college, and she'd agreed—but she didn't seem as excited as he'd expected. Then she broke up with him four months later and moved to Los Angeles, where she'd taken a job with a software company. He couldn't remember the details; all he heard was her voice saying, "I'm sorry, Joe. But I don't want to live on a ranch. I want more."

He still wondered if she'd ever truly loved him. If she had, then they could have worked something out. But instead, she'd picked concrete, high-rises and crowds over his Silver River Ranch.

And all his dreams went up in smoke.

He'd built up the Silver River Ranch in the hope he'd have a wife and kids to share it with, but obviously that wasn't in the cards. At least the ranch was solid and dependable. Women were flighty and fickle—and he wouldn't make the same mistake twice.

A crash brought him back to reality. It was Maggie, scared by Calico, his aunt's cat.

Luckily, it was only a suitcase that she had kicked over—it had hit the wooden floor with a solid smack. As Maggie scrambled to right it, he noticed that her hands were shaking.

She was nervous, and he didn't think that it was just the cat.

Was it *him?* Or the situation?

"Maggie, have you ever been on a ranch before?" he asked.

"No."

"Have you ever ridden a horse?"

"No."

"Are you scared to ride?" he asked. "Or just nervous?"

"A little of both." She bit her lip—the simple gesture made his blood heat for some reason.

"Okay, I'm *a lot* scared and a lot nervous. I'm scared of losing Danny to the system. I'm scared of the whole cattle drive. But mostly, I'm scared that Cowboy Quest won't be enough to help us fix what's broken."

Joe wanted to take Maggie's hand and assure her that everything would be okay, that Cowboy Quest was all about improving communication skills and team building, but he didn't dare touch her. Nor did he want to tell her that, from what he'd read, Maggie and Danny simply needed time together.

If she hadn't already figured that out, she would.

"Please don't worry, Maggie. Believe me, all your concerns will be addressed. If not, just come to me."

She closed her eyes and let out a long breath. "Thank you. That makes me feel much better. And I'll come to you for any help I may need. I really want to make the most out of your program."

"Perfect. That's just what I want to hear."

Then it dawned on him.

Since she was the first adult that he had in his program, and a woman at that, he'd have to make some concessions for her, like separate facilities and her own tent for the cattle drive. But he couldn't afford to make too many allowances for her lack of experience when he had a lot to accomplish before the cattle drive started.

Joe also knew that Maggie wasn't likely to confide in him too much. But he was sympathetic to Maggie's problems with Danny. He knew what was at stake for them both, and she had a darn good reason to worry.

Adding that to the fact that she needed to complete Cowboy Quest with Danny—and learn to ride, apparently—he definitely could empathize with what she was going through.

He'd do everything possible to help her.

He felt like he already knew her—at least, Maggie the performer. He knew she'd won a Tony award and had appeared in numerous musicals and even on TV.

He also knew things had been going fine with Danny up until his mother's death two years ago. Then Danny started running with a bad bunch of kids. The probation officer who investigated the situation felt that Maggie's rehearsal and performance schedule left Danny alone much too often, and that he needed more supervision.

On one of those nights when he'd snuck out of the apartment, Danny had been arrested.

In a phone call from his old college buddy, Judge

Pat Cunningham in New York City, Joe had learned that Maggie had to give up rehearsals for a new show in order to participate in Cowboy Quest. Pat felt bad about that, but knew that it was important for Maggie to spend time with Danny, to bond and rebuild the stable home environment he so desperately needed.

Her intentions were admirable, but Joe hoped that it wasn't too late. Why had she let things come to this?

"Look at all this counter space," Maggie said, running her hand along the emerald-green granite. "I never have much time to cook, but I love it. I tape all the cooking shows and try different recipes whenever I can."

Maggie suddenly froze in place, then slowly turned to him. "Whoa. Am I supposed to cook for everyone in the program?"

He stifled a smile. "Well, you said you liked to cook."

When her eyebrows shot up in shock, he chuckled. "I was just kidding. The ranch has a cook, and he always loves the challenge of a dozen more mouths to feed—a baker's dozen, counting you."

"Joe, am I the only parent or guardian who's participating?"

"Yes."

She looked like she was about to hit the panic button. "Just me?"

"We have other counseling components for family members set up post-Cowboy Quest, but you are it as far as an adult and as a female who's going to actually join the cattle drive." He grinned. "Twelve teenage boys, six cowboy counselors and you."

Maggie raised an eyebrow. "Why am I the only one?"

"Judge Cunningham asked me to make an exception for you, so I did. Now let me show you to your room."

"I'm sure it'll be fine."

And it was. He could tell that Maggie appreciated the view of the mountains from the guest bedroom, the balcony off the room with several lawn chairs and a table, the big log bed and the brightly striped Hudson's Bay blankets that he'd acquired over the years.

There were several items handed down from his grandparents—his mother's parents—that impressed her. He'd carefully preserved them in shadow boxes that he'd made and displayed them throughout the house.

His grandmother's baskets and several pieces of clothing with her original beadwork, medicine bags—none of it escaped Maggie's attention.

"And these photographs...fabulous." She seemed to be talking to herself, then she turned to him. "Who is the photographer?"

"My dad. My mother is a travel reporter, and my father was a rancher and a stock contractor. I learned the business from him. But on the day I graduated from college, he drove up the driveway with a mammoth motor home, handed me the keys to this house and said that all five thousand acres were mine—and he was going to see the world with my mom."

"Five thousand acres?" Her eyes grew wide. "He just walked away from all of this?"

"After I tried to talk him out of it, he confessed that he liked being on the road and seeing the world with my mother, that he'd grown tired of the ranch. And of course my mother was thrilled."

He'd thought three people loved the ranch as much as he did—Ellen and his parents.

Damn, had he been wrong!

And what was wrong with his judgment of people?

The ranch meant everything to him. It was the reason he woke up every morning and the reason he went to bed exhausted each night. He knew every blade of grass, every animal and every tree on the property. It was his life's blood.

Someone like Maggie could never understand that, so he wouldn't even try explaining it to her.

"I'll let you get settled then," Joe said, then eyed her fancy blouse, slacks and strappy shoes. "I hope you brought some work clothes. If you'd like to change into something warmer, I'll give you a quick tour of the ranch before the sun sets."

"I'd like that."

"I'll wait for you in the living room."

He settled into his favorite overstuffed chair and prepared to wait a long while for Miss Broadway, but to his surprise she appeared just a handful of minutes later. Obviously she was used to quick costume changes.

And change she had. Her dark blue jeans fit her snugly in all the right places. A pastel plaid blouse and a sparkly belt topped off her outfit, and it looked like she had on brand-new black cowboy boots.

He gave a long whistle. "You look like you're ready to go out on the town. You're dressed a little too fancy for Cowboy Quest."

"Oh." She shook her head. "My whole wardrobe is like this. I bought out Bloomingdale's."

"Maybe you could go shopping."

"There are department stores here?"

"Sure. The Mountain Springs Feed and Sundries has a whole bunch of clothes next to the fertilizer and tractor parts." He winked.

She laughed. "Let's go."

"You think I'm kidding?"

"I hope you are." She picked up Calico and rubbed his ears. The cat snuggled up against her neck, pushing and rubbing her head against Maggie.

The pure pleasure on Maggie's face tugged at his heart, yet it troubled him to see the sadness in her eyes.

"We'll get to be good friends, Calico. Won't we?" she asked.

Calico purred his agreement.

"I've always wanted a pet," she said. "But my schedule just doesn't…" She scratched the cat's ears. "I can't even take care of Danny."

"Yes, you can," Joe said. "Don't be so hard on yourself. You've both been through a terrible loss—it takes time to adjust."

The lost look in her eyes made him want to take her into his arms, but Joe forced himself to get back to business.

"We'll use the golf cart and follow the Silver River," Joe said.

"Sounds good to me."

A few minutes later, when she settled in next to him in the golf cart, he caught the scent of some floral perfume that suited her perfectly. The light breeze tossed her blond hair around her face, and he liked it when it brushed his shoulder. Too soon, she restrained it with some kind of clip.

He reminded himself again that this was business, not pleasure and that thinking about her perfume and hair wasn't appropriate.

To make matters worse, the ground wasn't level here—it was a jarring ride. Maggie kept bumping into him, not that he minded, and every now and then she'd shoot him an embarrassed glance.

Joe pulled up alongside of the river and drove slower. "Do you have any questions about the program?"

She looked straight ahead and he heard her inhale. "My only priority is making sure that Danny is okay. The other thing I need to do is to help him satisfactorily complete your program or he's headed for placement in a juvenile facility, and I don't want that." She took a deep breath, and bit down on her bottom lip. "And I'm supposed to come up with some kind of plan for better supervision of Danny when we get back home and a way to spend more time with him. That'll be a challenge. If I could have found a better plan, I would have instituted it."

That lost look crept into her eyes again. "You'll come up with something, Maggie. Maybe I can help."

Joe knew that he had been given a lot of power over her and her relationship with Danny, and if he were Maggie, he wouldn't like it either.

"It's going to be hard trusting anyone with Danny," she continued. "You see, I've had custody of him for the past two years. You've known him for—what?—twelve seconds?"

"I understand your concern. I do. But Cowboy Quest met with one hundred percent success the first time. This is our second run."

"Define success," she said, suddenly cooler.

"On paper, I'd say success would be all the boys completing all the requirements. But what I'd really want would be for them to use the components of it—the practical and character lessons—for a lifetime."

She crossed her fingers. "I really hope that happens."

"Me, too."

"I read in your pamphlet that you have a master's degree in special education," she said.

"With a minor in psychology."

She folded her arms in front of her. "And those cowboys in the bunkhouse? What are their credentials?"

"Believe it or not, a couple of them have graduate degrees, most have bachelor degrees, but more importantly, they are good men and good role models. And they care about each and every kid."

"That's good to hear," she said. "How did you get into this, Joe?"

He rubbed his chin. Where to start? "My own father wasn't around much when I was growing up. Either he was busy hauling livestock around the country, or he was traveling with my mother, taking photos for travel books. If it weren't for Mr. Dixon— my pal Jake's dad—I would have been placed in a juvenile correctional facility and never let out.

He helped me in more ways than one. I guess I'm paying that back."

He was worried about his program this time around. He had shared with his staff that the twelve boys they were getting seemed more difficult than the first group, and they all had a history of running away, including Danny. They'd all have to be extra vigilant.

But he was going to think positively. He had a good team.

"And if someone fails to complete the program?"

"No one has yet." Joe studied her. Her brows were almost touching, and her hands were clasped tightly on her lap.

"But you've only had one run of Cowboy Quest so far. Danny's future hinges on an almost untested program."

"I suppose you could put it that way." He met her worried look. "But Cowboy Quest has been under a lot of scrutiny from the state and county. It's being studied as a model for other, similar programs."

Her lips were pinched now, and she was looking away from him. She was definitely anxious.

"Maggie, don't worry. Cowboy Quest is not about the riding or the livestock. It's about problem solving, maturing and working as a team. We use the Cowboy Code as a guide for basic rules of living. So don't worry. The boys and I will do everything possible to get everyone through the program with flying colors."

Her grass-green eyes pooled with unshed tears and once again he felt the urge to comfort her.

The only reason he'd send in a negative report to Judge Cunningham on Maggie and Danny was if they didn't make *some* attempt to resolve their issues, but he wasn't going to tell her that yet. He needed to wait and see just how things played out, and just how hard Danny and Maggie worked on their relationship and solving the problems between them, logistical and otherwise.

From what he could see, Danny was a thirteen-year-old who couldn't be trusted to attend school and not run the street.

Maggie was trying to work and support the two of them, in a job with horrible hours, and in his current state, Danny needed more—if not constant—supervision. He needed a *parent*.

Somehow in all that there needed to be a plan for their future together, or they would spend their future apart.

"Remember, Maggie, I have a vested interest in making sure that all the participants are successful. We have a good program here—but we're under a lot of scrutiny from the state. I don't want to give them any excuses to shut us down."

"So you might lose your program, and I might lose custody of Danny." Maggie took a deep breath. "Then we'd both better make Cowboy Quest a success."

Chapter Three

Maggie tried to stay optimistic as she leaned back against the cushioned seat of the golf cart and watched the sun set over the rugged, snow-capped mountains in the distance. A sweet, unfamiliar heat washed over her. She was sure that it was caused by her new tour guide's hard, muscular thigh pressed lightly against hers.

She enjoyed listening to Joe talk about his ranch. She could hear the pride in his voice when he pointed out which animal won Bull of the Year from the Professional Bull Riders Association and which ones were up and coming.

But she couldn't forget how much power Joe had

over her. With one report to the judge, she might lose Danny forever. And here they were, both fish out of water, trying to fit into a program that they didn't have a clue about.

But as Joe said, it wasn't about the livestock or the riding. That they could probably muddle through with a little luck and a lot of help. It was the bonding between her and Danny that was going to be the hardest. There was a lot of hurt between them. But she had faith in Danny. She'd loved him since he was born, and she still did. Somewhere in that teenage mess was the Danny who loved her back.

As they neared a hillside pasture, she could see the silhouettes of bulls grazing in the distance. Beautiful horses graced the corral; more were in a lower pasture.

"Would you like to see the barn?" he asked.

"Sure." Actually, she really didn't. She wanted to curl up somewhere and sleep. It had been a long traveling day.

He pulled up to the corral and several horses came to inspect them. He took a bag of sugar cubes from the glove compartment and handed some to her. "Keep your hand flat. You don't want to lose any fingers." He jumped out of the vehicle and led her into the barn.

Lights blazed inside. As Joe walked past the stalls, he called all the horses by name, and she petted them.

"You sure look at home in a barn, Maggie."

"As it happens, I grew up on a dairy farm in northern New York."

His eyes grew as wide as his belt buckle. "Well, I'll be. And here I had you pegged as a bona fide city slicker."

"Hang on. I *am* a city slicker. I've lived in Manhattan longer than I lived on my parents' farm. Besides, I didn't particularly like it. My sister, Liz, was the one who loved it."

"And Danny is Liz's son."

"Yes." Even though Liz had been gone for two years, Maggie missed her every day. Danny looked a lot like her.

"And you think you've failed Liz because Danny is in trouble," Joe said, pausing with a bucket of water for the next horse in line.

"Was that in the probation report, too?"

He nodded. "It said something to the effect that you felt like you failed Liz because Danny was arrested."

Maggie felt like she was under a microscope.

He was here to run Cowboy Quest—not to analyze her. She was here to save her nephew. End of story.

They got back into the golf cart. Ominous clouds had darkened the sky, and the breeze had grown rough and cool. "What's Danny doing now?" she asked, changing the subject.

"Ronnie is giving him a tour like I'm giving you. If the other participants have arrived, they are all touring together."

"Danny's probably hungry," Maggie said, her own stomach giving a little growl. "It's been a long day, and he didn't eat much."

"He'll be fine." Joe checked his watch. "Dinner is in an hour."

Just as they pulled up to the ranch house, the skies opened with a crack of thunder. Rain came down in a noisy torrent. They dashed inside. Joe lit a fire in the living room and they sat to warm themselves.

"You know a lot about me, Joe. Tell me more about yourself," she said.

"There isn't much to tell." He shrugged. "I was a fairly mediocre student in high school. My parents weren't around much then so I practically moved into Jake Dixon's house. It was Mr. Dixon who suggested that I could work my ranch, expand my stock contracting business and still do something with my master's in education. One day, I came up with the idea for Cowboy Quest."

He paused and diverted his eyes, clearly uncomfortable talking about himself.

"Don't stop," Maggie urged.

"Jake Dixon, our pal Clint Scully and I all help out on Jake's Gold Buckle Ranch. He runs several programs for kids during the summer, so Cowboy

Quest fits right in. Mr. and Mrs. Dixon handle most of the administrative duties."

"And you handle the program part," Maggie stated.

He nodded. "The three of us go way back to Mountain Springs Grammar School. After high school, we rodeoed together for years. The only one still chasing rodeos is Clint."

"So what does a stock contractor actually do?"

"I furnish rodeo stock for rodeos—steers, broncs, bulls, calves. I breed them, too—buy, sell, trade."

"Sounds like hard work, raising all those animals."

"I'm not afraid of hard work." He smiled. "And that's another component of the Cowboy Code. If we can get these boys up and working, they'll be too tired to think of getting into trouble, and at the end of the day, they can take pride in what they've accomplished. I hope that learning the value of hard work will stay with them when they go back home."

"*If* you can get them working."

"Oh, I will. Starting with dinner tonight." He tipped his hat, excused himself and added, "I'll see you in a half hour."

As Maggie walked to the bunkhouse, she caught the scent of horses again, heavy on the breeze.

She did some breathing exercises—she always

did when she was nervous. Only a handful of people knew that she suffered from stage fright, but now she was suffering from horse fright. She'd been dreading tomorrow, but the sight of the horses reminded her: riding lessons tomorrow.

She told herself that it'd be okay. She'd seen horses before, pulling carriages around Central Park. The tourists petted, posed and took pictures with them and they were as still as statutes.

But the Silver River Ranch was totally different from New York.

Here there were *real* horses. Horses that she'd be riding...in a saddle...by herself. And they were tall. It was a long way to the ground if she fell.

Maggie paused to check her way. She'd forgotten how dark it could be at night in the country. There weren't any streetlights, brightly illuminated office buildings or Broadway marquees to guide the way, and she could barely see the path in front of her. She stopped to let her eyes send a message to her brain, sorting out the shadows and shapes.

Then she made out the tall figure of Joe Watley approaching, carrying a flashlight. Relief washed over her as he called out.

"I thought this would help." She heard a click, and he handed her a flashlight of her own. "Keep it while you're here."

"Thanks."

The bunkhouse was aglow in the distance, and it

looked warm and welcoming. She took another deep breath, and pushed thoughts of tomorrow aside.

"What's for dinner?" she asked as they walked.

"Cookie's mystery stew."

"Shall I ask about the name, or don't I want to know?"

"He makes it different each time. One of the cowboys called it that, and the name stuck. The meat he uses is a mystery, too."

"Ouch."

They both laughed, and Maggie warmed to his sense of humor. Yet being with Joe—the whole situation—made her jumpy. If they walked in together, it would be like admitting that he was spending extra time with her.

Sure enough, when they entered, they were greeted with a moment of hushed silence. Then the talking and frivolity began again in earnest.

She noticed Danny right away, along with the poke in the ribs that the big kid on his right gave him. Danny winced, and so did Maggie. She clamped her lips together and took a seat at the head of the table, next to Joe—the only two seats left.

Everyone seemed to have been waiting for her to arrive before they ate, and she vowed that she'd never be tardy again. She checked her watch—five after six. She was only five minutes late.

Joe cleared his throat. "Gentlemen and Maggie,

let's take a minute to reflect silently on the bounty of the meal and the opportunity to be in Cowboy Quest." He bowed his head.

Emulating Joe, the cowboys removed their hats and put them over their hearts. It took a moment before the boys in the program decided what to do, but eventually they bowed their heads—everyone but Danny, the smallest kid in the program, and his newfound friend, the biggest kid in the program. They smirked.

Joe spoke quietly. "Heavenly Father, thank you for this food which we are about to eat, and may everyone around this table get what they can out of Cowboy Quest, and more. God bless us all and keep us safe. Amen."

"Amen," echoed most everyone around the table.

A warmth, like a plush blanket, enveloped her. She remembered sitting around her parents' big oak table as they all bowed their heads to pray. As they ate, they'd discuss current events, school, the weather—anything and everything in between.

These days she always ate on the run—stopping at the deli next to her condo, or for Chinese take-out somewhere, or for a quick slice of pizza. Max's delivered, so she'd arrange for Danny to have most of his meals from there.

She hired a housekeeper, a math and reading tutor and got him a membership to the gym down the street. They went to counselors. She did everything she possibly could to help Danny, but she still wished she could have given more of herself.

Now, even though there were two dozen other people at the table, she was sharing a meal with Danny for a change.

Speaking of meals, Cookie's mystery meal was stew, and it was fabulous, loaded with carrots and potatoes.

Ronnie tapped on his coffee mug with a spoon. "Let's all go around the table and introduce ourselves."

After all the introductions were made, Maggie noticed that Danny and she were the only ones who came from the east coast. All the rest, including staff, were from either the west or southwest.

No surprise there.

Maggie found out that Danny's new friend was named Brandon Avery and he was from Billings, Montana.

As she stifled a yawn, Joe stood again. "Since this was a long day of travel, everyone will help with the cleanup. The Cowboy Quest participants will hit the hay ahead of schedule tonight because tomorrow morning will come early, five-thirty, to be exact. We have stock to feed and water, stalls to muck out and then you all will be taking riding lessons after your school lessons. Let me stress once again that you'll get out of the program what you put into it—so give it your all."

"He's getting free labor out of this. So, like, how many juvenile delinquents does it take to run a ranch?"

The guffaws and tittering washed over her like a tidal wave. She couldn't believe Danny would be that rude.

"Danny, you shouldn't—" Maggie began.

Joe held up a hand like a traffic cop, and she got his message: He was in charge.

"I've heard that before," Joe said. "So I'm glad that you cleared the air, Dan. But if you really believe that I'm getting free labor out of this, well, then, I'd better fire all these cowboys, huh? After all, I won't need them because I have the twelve of you."

This time it was the cowboys who laughed and snickered. The boys looked somewhat awkward, as did Danny and his new friend.

Maggie checked her watch. Seven o'clock. If she went to bed at eight, she'd have over eight hours of sleep. That was definitely more than she got in a typical night.

She was exhausted. Danny looked dead on his feet, too.

There was no way that she was going to be late on her first day, even if she was scared out of her mind. No way.

"I'm going to walk Miss McIntyre to the ranch house," Joe said. "Then I'll be right back to help in the cleanup."

She wondered if Joe had stressed that for the rest of the participants, or just for Danny.

Maggie sighed. In spite of the fact that Joe wanted to handle things, she had to find the time to talk to her nephew, to alleviate his concerns.

And make sure he didn't blow their last chance.

Joe walked Maggie up the brick walkway to the main house, the glow of their flashlights combining to illuminate the way.

He'd had an enjoyable meal with everyone, but particularly Maggie. He'd even arranged to take her into Mountain Springs tomorrow for some real Western wear. She needed cowboy boots— *real* boots—not those fluff designer shoes she'd brought.

He'd already received a heads-up from Quint that Danny's clothes weren't proper for ranch work, either. They were okay for a gangster, but there'd be none of that for the young Daniel Turner.

"I'm sorry I jumped in earlier, Joe."

"That's okay. I'm sure it's difficult to make the adjustment from aunt and primary caretaker to just one of the guys."

"Yeah, it's hard." She shook her head. "As you

can tell, Danny's got a problem with peer pressure. He'll say or do anything for a laugh."

"I know. I've seen it time and time again. Give me and my staff a little credit, Maggie, and trust in Danny a little more."

"I've trusted Danny in the past. You can see where it got me."

"But today is a new day."

She knew Joe was right. She had to back off and calm down.

But it was too darn difficult when she was so desperate to help Danny.

"I'm sure it's much easier if there were two parents to help raise kids." She sighed. "Are you married?"

He was quiet for a moment. "No, I've never been married. I was engaged once, but it didn't work out."

He took a breath. "Look, Maggie, I've volunteered for the programs at the Gold Buckle Ranch for eight years now. And, yeah, I have a degree, but what I also have is a clean slate and an unbiased point of view. I can look at things more objectively than you."

She supposed he was right. "So what have you objectively figured out about me and Danny so far?"

"Well, right now, I'd point out that you aren't

going to be around to fight Danny's battles all the time. He needs the skills to stand up to his peers."

She hadn't done a great job so far, but she had to perform eight shows a week. It was her job. She'd imposed on friends and sometimes hired the best people she could to keep an eye on Danny while she worked, but he still kept sneaking out on them, claiming that he didn't need "no stinkin' babysitter." And that he wasn't a baby.

"Okay, Joe. I'll do it your way, and I'll keep quiet, and let you handle things. But just be advised that being quiet is not one of my virtues."

They walked the rest of the way in silence. At the house, Joe let Maggie open the door and turn on the lights.

"All okay?" he asked. She seemed a little nervous tonight. Maybe she just didn't want to stay by herself in a strange house. He wished Aunt Betty hadn't gone out of town. She could have kept Maggie company.

"I'm okay," she said. "But it's so quiet here. How am I ever going to sleep?"

"I can fix you a place in the barn if you'd like. It can get pretty noisy out there." He winked.

"Uh…no…" She laughed. "But thanks anyway."

Maggie looked so very…kissable. The dim hallway light made her golden hair shimmer. He longed to run his hand through her blond locks, to pull her to him....

A laugh from the bunkhouse brought him back to reality. What was he thinking? She was a participant in his program.

"Um...good night, Joe."

"'Night, Maggie." He headed down the path, then stopped. "The phone number to the bunkhouse is right by the phone. Call if you need anything— anything at all."

He gritted his teeth. That sounded like a proposition, and he hadn't meant that at all.

"I mean...uh..." He couldn't think.

"I know what you mean, Joe. See you bright and early."

She smiled, and the door closed.

He caught himself whistling as he walked to the bunkhouse. He hadn't whistled in ages.

But sleep wouldn't come. He kept thinking about Maggie, who had a wagonload of trouble she had to deal with. Her heaviest cargo was the smallest kid in Cowboy Quest.

Would he be able to help her?

Tossing and turning, he thought about his growing attraction to Maggie and how he had to resist. It would be unprofessional, and a huge complication.

He had a highly charged program to run, loaded with high-risk juveniles with emotional issues and one interesting woman who was constantly intruding on his thoughts.

How was he going to keep his mind on business?

Chapter Four

Maggie barely slept. She kept having dreams of falling off horses as tall as the Empire State Building.

Four-thirty came way too early. She grabbed the clothes that she'd laid out last night and hurried to the shower.

At five o'clock sharp, she was at the barn, shivering in her designer coat. She could see the cowboys and the kids walking in single file up the hill. Joe led the way, his long strides determined and purposeful. Danny lagged behind the group with Brandon.

She hoped that the two of them didn't get too

close. Danny was a first-class follower. He was the type of kid that others liked to egg on, then sit back and watch him take the fall.

Maybe Cowboy Quest would teach him how to be a leader.

"Morning, Maggie," Joe said, handing her a mug of steaming coffee.

"Morning."

He also handed her a flannel shirt. "I brought you this. I figured you'd need it."

Judging by the size, it was one of his.

"We might need to move up our shopping trip to after breakfast." Joe said, nodding in Danny's direction. "It's cold here until about noon or so. You both need warmer clothes."

It looked as though Danny was wearing all the contents of his suitcase. The other kids were dressed appropriately. Obviously, they knew more than she.

"I think you're right." She hurriedly took off her coat and slipped into Joe's flannel shirt. It was so soft and comfortable, and she caught the scent of laundry soap and his spicy aftershave. She buttoned it up, rolled up the sleeves and put her coat back on. His shirt hung almost to her knees, but she was much warmer, and grateful.

She looked at the horses milling around the corral. Now when she shivered, it wasn't from the cold. It was pure fright.

Quint took charge, and they all worked in teams of three to water and feed the horses and muck the stalls. Maggie, Danny and Ronnie were a team. She liked the big cowboy with the shaggy blond hair and the easy smile. While Maggie bit her tongue, Ronnie deftly deflected any negative remarks that Danny made.

By the time they'd fed and watered their allotment of horses, mucked their fair share of stalls and turned out some horses into the corral, the sun was rising over the mountains.

Maggie couldn't stop herself from looking at Joe. His unique laugh and sense of humor never failed to make her smile. She watched as he swung big bales of hay as if they were nothing but a handful of feathers. She sneaked a glance as he patiently instructed one of the boys as to the correct way to lay down fresh hay.

There was some grumbling, refusals to work, talk about slave labor and talk about how they were feeling punished. Joe took the worst complainers aside and had a heart-to-heart with them. Danny was the first to be invited to talk to Joe. He returned to the group a little quieter, more contemplative.

Finally, they all headed to the bunkhouse for breakfast. One of the boys, Cody, held the door open for her, and she smiled her thanks. He smiled back.

Danny was already inside and sitting at the table,

but when Joe checked his clipboard and called Danny's name to help Cookie, he got up with only a bit of eye rolling.

Joe took a seat opposite Maggie. When Danny brought out platters of scrambled eggs, pancakes and sausages and laid them on the table, no one made a move to help themselves.

This time, Quint said the prayer. When it was over, everything was passed, and there was a minimum of talking. When the platters were empty, Danny got up from his seat and took them to Cookie for a refill. Clearly, he was already making some progress.

After breakfast, Joe announced that it was time for classes and individual tutoring so they could keep up with their schoolwork, and that she and Danny would be going into town with him for supplies.

This brought a couple of stupid grins from the boys in the program and the words "suck up" reached her ears. Danny's face flushed pink with humiliation, and he was about to spew something back, but he held his tongue.

Peers could be brutal, and Maggie wondered how Danny would be able to live with the taunts. Maybe he could learn to deal with them—with Joe's help.

Joe enjoyed watching Maggie as he drove into Mountain Springs. She seemed truly enthralled by the beauty of the surrounding terrain—the snow-capped peaks in the distance, the wildflowers along the road. Or maybe she was just having a nervous reaction to being so far out of her element, away from the hectic city she seemed to love.

Danny wasn't talking. He ostensibly slept in the backseat, but every now and then Joe could see his eyes flutter open. He was definitely watching them carefully.

Oblivious to her nephew's subterfuge, Maggie kept up a steady stream of chatter.

"I'm really sorry that you have to take the time to take us shopping, Joe. I thought I'd brought the correct items."

"Danny just needs a couple pair of jeans that don't drag on the ground. And you said that you bought dude ranch clothes for yourself. They'll do, but they're awfully fancy, so you might want to get some casual things. Plus, you both need warmer clothes for the cattle drive." He rubbed his chin. "Didn't you get a clothing list from Mrs. Dixon, Jake's mom?"

"Uh…I probably did. I have a pile of mail I didn't get a chance to look at, but I brought it with me." She paused. "I'm normally not this disorganized, but everything went just so fast, and—"

"I understand." But he didn't. Who wouldn't open their mail on a daily basis or bring the correct clothes for a Wyoming cattle drive in late spring?

"Don't worry. We'll take care of getting you both some appropriate things to wear."

Once they parked in town and stepped inside Mountain Springs Feed and Sundries, Maggie was overwhelmed.

"This is totally amazing! I've never seen a place like this."

It was indeed a mishmash of everything under the sun. Chicken feed was positioned near wallpaper, house paint was a step away from barbed wire and rodent traps were near barbecue supplies. Joe supposed there was some logic to the place, but it escaped him.

Maggie seemed astonished that the clothing was in the middle of the store, right next to a restaurant that was doing a booming business. She was even more amazed that if she wanted to try something on there were no dressing rooms *per se*. She was directed to a display of tents in the back of the store doubling as dressing rooms.

But Maggie didn't complain. She sported an amused smile and good-naturedly tried on clothing inside the tent while Danny sat on a nearby bench, a sour expression on his face.

"Are these jeans okay?" she asked Joe moments later, pulling open the tent flap.

Joe's mouth suddenly went dry. He'd seen rodeo queens with looser jeans. He took a breath. "They look…fine."

Rolling his eyes, Danny finally got up and moved to the six-person orange-and-tan tent opposite Maggie. Hopefully, he was trying on his jeans.

"Dan? How are you doing?" Joe asked.

"These jeans are lame," came the muffled answer.

"Mind if I have a look?" Joe asked.

"Whatever."

Joe popped into the tent. The jeans fit him perfectly. Then Danny tried to tug them down low on his hips.

"Look, Dan. I can't have you dragging your pants. First, it's too dangerous around here. I don't want the cuffs getting stuck in the stirrups. Second, there's no one here you need to impress. You can be yourself."

Danny nodded. He didn't seem to fight it all that much, and Joe wondered about that.

That's when Joe saw the bulge in the pocket of Danny's old pants. A black handle showed, and the knife had to be at least six inches long.

Joe shook his head. "Did you intend to buy the knife that's in your pants pocket there?" He whispered so Maggie wouldn't overhear.

Danny's eyes went to the object. Then he met Joe's gaze, as if daring Joe to say more.

Joe met the challenge. "I didn't think so. If you need a knife for the trail, I'll buy you one. Besides, stealing is against—"

"The Cowboy Code," Danny said sarcastically.

Joe nodded. "So put it back."

The boy at least had enough sense to look embarrassed and maybe a bit sorry.

"Are you going to tell my aunt?"

"Should I?"

"Nah. She'll just yell, or cry. Sometimes I hear her crying." He bit down on his lower lip, as if he said too much.

"Why is she crying, Dan? Over you?"

The boy shrugged. "I guess so."

Joe shook his head. "She cares about you. She loves you." Danny gave a slight nod. "We'll keep the knife thing between us as long as you don't do it again."

"Are you going to send me home?" He raised an eyebrow, and Joe thought that the kid actually wanted to be sent home.

"Not a chance, Dan. The only way that I'll send you home is if you are a success. If you fail, you'll go right into placement at a juvenile correctional facility," Joe said, knowing that he would do his damnedest not to let that happen.

Danny's lip curled, but Joe could see the despair in the boy's eyes. "My aunt must have told me a thousand times that I'm going to be placed if I blow this. I'm sick of hearing it."

"Than why would you do a dumb thing like stealing that knife?"

He shrugged, but he took the knife and handed it to Joe.

Joe flipped it around in his hand. "I'll never mention placement again, as long as you don't do anything dumb like that again." Joe held out his hand. "Deal?"

Danny shook his hand, but the pinched expression on his face told him that Danny didn't like being forced into a promise.

"Deal," he finally said.

"Good. Now let's buy both you and your aunt cowboy hats."

Danny shrugged, but a slight smile tugged at the corner of his lips. Seems like a cowboy hat wasn't lame, but cool.

Any of the guys could have taught Maggie how to ride, but Joe wanted to do it, so he put himself into the schedule.

He knew he should stay focused on his program, and not Maggie, but he told himself that she was a member of his program and the one who needed the most individual training.

They walked up the hill to the barn together. On the way, he explained the process, to make her more at ease.

"We have two days to give you a basic knowledge of bridling, saddling and horse care in preparation for the cattle drive on Wednesday. Plus, we need to keep up with our regular chores."

"Who's going to do the chores when we're on the cattle drive?" Maggie asked.

"A bunch of volunteers from Jake Dixon's Gold Buckle Ranch. We help each other out." He smiled. "Wait here. I'll be right out."

Joe went into the barn and brought out Lady for Maggie. Lady was a gentle and patient soul who took the bit easily.

Maggie backed up and gave Lady a wide berth.

"That's a big horse," she said, eyes wide. "A really big horse."

Joe knew that Maggie was apprehensive about riding, but now he wondered if she was in fact afraid—which would make the cattle drive even more difficult for her. She was okay in the barn where the horses were secured in their stalls, but on the trail, her fear could be dangerous—unless he was able to help her overcome it.

"Maggie, this is Lady. She's a horse that we rescued from some very bad conditions."

He handed Maggie some sugar cubes. "Put them flat on your hand like I showed you. She'll like you immediately."

The horse gently took the cubes from Maggie's hand.

"Lady wouldn't hurt a flea. I picked her out just for you. The two of you will do fine."

He and Maggie shared a gaze. He saw the relief on her face, and he felt a stab of warmth deep in his gut.

He wanted her to be happy and enjoy riding, but the importance he placed on both was a puzzle that he couldn't figure out. Why was it so important to him?

Her tried not to stare at her lush lips that made him want to kiss away any lingering fear. Cast his gaze away from her twinkling green eyes. He had work to do.

As time went on, Maggie became more comfortable with Lady and mastered bridling and saddling the horse to his satisfaction.

Finally, Joe knew that he had to end the lesson. It was getting too damn difficult to ignore the pull of awareness when his hand touched hers, to watch her worry her bottom lip when she was concentrating.

Those lips. The lips that he wanted to kiss.

Maybe it would be better for him to assign Maggie to another one of the cowboys... No. He had to do it. He'd taught several people who were nervous to ride a horse, but she was by far the jumpiest of the bunch. He wanted to personally make sure that she didn't startle Lady—she had to learn to control the animal, as well as her anxiety.

Soon it was time for lunch. After lunch, he'd give Maggie her first riding lesson.

He'd teach her to ride, no problem. But he didn't know what to do about the attraction that was threatening to distract him from his goal.

Chapter Five

"Let's get back to the corral, Maggie," Joe said after lunch. "We need to work on your fear of riding."

And she'd thought she was doing such a good job of hiding her fear today.

Busted.

She glanced over at Danny. Judging by the scowl on his face, he hadn't missed a word of Joe's invitation. She'd have to talk to him later, reassure him that nothing was going on.

"Sure," she answered.

Joe didn't say a word until they walked to a wooden bench along a slight bend in the Silver

River. He gestured to the bench and she took a seat. He sat down next to her.

"You're more scared of riding than I thought," he said bluntly. "You worked around them just fine, but being too nervous about riding increases your chances of getting hurt. We've got to help you control your fear."

"I actually thought that I'd be okay. But seeing them up close and personal, without them being in a stall—" She shivered.

He took a seat next to her. "All the horses have been especially picked out and trained for Cowboy Quest. So put your mind at ease. With practice, you'll get better and better and more relaxed. Okay?"

His voice and demeanor were so gentle, she wanted to be successful for him…er…for *Danny* and for herself.

"I'm not one to back away from a challenge. I'm giving this my best shot. Just let me have a moment before we start so I can do my breathing exercises. That always helps me."

"What else are you afraid of that you have to do breathing exercises?"

"I get pretty bad stage fright—stress, actually. And this is stress personified."

"I'll give you whatever time you need, Maggie. And I never thought you'd back away, not for a moment. If you can perform on Broadway before a huge crowd and go on TV to accept your Tony and make a speech, then riding Lady should be like...uh..."

"Riding the carousel in Central Park?"

"Easier." He took her hand, studied it and then released it. He was gentle, then his face became impassive. She'd love to know what he was thinking just then.

"I'm okay now. Go ahead," she said, inhaling and exhaling deeply. "I'll meet you at the barn."

"If you're sure." He stood and headed back toward the barn.

"Joe?"

He turned back and waited.

She exhaled loudly. "Thanks."

He gave her the thumbs-up sign, along with a sexy wink.

But she wondered what he thought about her weakness, needing breathing exercises to cope with stress. Then it hit her. What if he thought she couldn't cope with Danny?

She couldn't let her defenses down like she had. From now on, she wasn't going to reveal any more of herself than necessary.

Maggie studied Lady in her stall. She looked harmless, even cute. Okay. This was girl-to-girl, *mano a mano*, ladies' night out, happy hour.

"Just don't throw me, Lady. I have a brilliant career going—or at least I *had* a brilliant career," she whispered. "I can't afford to break anything. I'm a dancer." She did a little two-step, humming to accompany herself.

Someone laughed, and she spun around. It was Joe. Her heart did a little leap in her chest at the sight of him.

"Lady likes it when someone sings to her."

"Good. I'll do *Phantom of the Opera.* Or maybe something from *Oklahoma!*" She chuckled.

"What about something from *Hearts and Flowers*?"

Her heart sank at the mere mention of the musical that she'd never get to do.

"How did you know the name of the show that I was—"

"The probation report."

"Ah…yes. That document is as comprehensive as the Declaration of Independence, isn't it?" she asked.

He grinned. "More."

She was getting lost in his eyes, then guilt set in. She looked around for Danny.

"I assigned Danny to another staff member," he said without her even asking. "I decided that you needed extra instruction."

Butterflies settled in her stomach. What would Danny think about her spending time—alone—with Joe?

"Maggie, do you resent having to come here and not being able to rehearse for your new musical?"

She tried to swallow the lump in her throat. "I don't want to talk about it. I'm here for a riding lesson."

"You're here for much more," he said softly.

She needed to get away from Cowboy Quest—to get away from him. She needed to think, but that was impossible right now. She had to do the right thing—no, she *wanted* to do the right thing—for Danny's sake.

She'd thought that maybe the right thing would be to quit performing and teach dance and voice. She'd done that with kids during the past few summers as part of a special theater program, and she'd loved it. But even if she did it full-time, she doubted that it would pay enough to support them both.

She petted Lady's nose as she sorted out the many things that were swirling around in her head.

"Maggie, you've got to talk to me—I want to help you, and Danny, but I can't unless you let me in."

"I know you're only trying to help, not pry, but I'm not comfortable relating my feelings to a person that I've only known for two days."

"Look—"

She couldn't hold it in any longer. "What do you want me to say? That I'm mad because I had to pass up the best role of my career to come here? That I feel guilty about feeling resentful toward Danny even though it's my fault that he screwed up? And if we are really psychoanalyzing me, I resent my sister Liz for dying, and not being here for Danny." Her hands shook, and she stuffed them into her pockets. "So the short answer is *yes*. I *do* resent having to come here."

She kicked a loose stone into the river. "Wow. Just how horrible am I?"

"Tell me about Liz. Why do you resent her for dying?"

Tears stung Maggie's eyes, and she blinked them back, willing them not to fall. "Because I miss her every day of my life. I want to talk to her one last time. I want to tell her how much I love her, and how much she's always meant to me. I want to tell her that I'm sorry that I let her down, that I've messed things up with Danny."

Tears fell down her cheeks and onto her blouse. She sniffed and fished in her pockets for some tissues. Joe handed her a folded red bandanna. "Sorry. I didn't mean to fall apart." But she had, and it felt like a giant weight had lifted off her chest. She'd thought these things often enough, but it was the first time she'd voiced them aloud. She hadn't even said this much to her grief counselor, but here on a wooden bench in Mountain Springs, Wyoming, she bared her soul to a cowboy.

"Cry all you want," Joe said. "It's good for you to get all this out in the open."

She managed to smile. "Thanks for listening, Joe."

"Everything you've said is all very understandable, Maggie." He shrugged. "You're only human, you know." He leaned forward, rested his arm on his knees and looked intently at her. "Now that we're talking, want to tell me why you're so scared of riding?"

She took a deep breath. "Okay. Here goes." She took several deep breaths and let them out. "My girlfriends and I would always save our babysitting money so we could ride at the stable by my house. The stable was about two miles away, and we'd ride our bikes there. This one time, someone else had reserved the horse that I always rode, the one I was used to."

She paused and smiled, thinking of her favorite horse. "His name was Sparky, and he was black and very sweet and gentle. Instead, I got a horse named Banner, a palomino, who was a nervous type, which didn't sit well with me because I wasn't the most confident rider." She shook her head. "The trainer who led us through the trails and across the farm fields thought it would be fun to jump a ditch that contained some irrigation equipment."

Joe grunted. "I know what's coming."

"Well, everyone soared over it, except me. I pulled on Banner's reins at the last second, and I went over his head and landed on my back on some kind of pipe." She closed her eyes. "He didn't step on me, but he came close. I remember seeing his underbelly. I got the wind knocked out of me. I couldn't breathe."

She was breathing hard now, reliving the incident. "Everyone was too busy laughing to notice that I couldn't breathe. Everything started to go dark around the edges, and their laughter seemed to get farther and farther away due to my lack of oxygen. I hit the ground and broke my arm. Luckily, as I fell again, it knocked something in place, and I could breathe again."

"What a horrible experience." Joe met her gaze. "Did you get back on?"

"No. I walked to the barn, got my bicycle and rode home using only my good arm. I never talked to my so-called friends again, and never went near a horse again." She smiled. "I'm even leery of the ones that pull carriages in New York City."

"No wonder you're scared, Maggie. Damn. Who wouldn't be? And you came here knowing that you had to ride."

"What else could I do? This is about Danny, not me. Keeping him out of placement is the issue, not my fear of horses." She crossed her fingers, and held them up. "I'm still hoping to overcome my fear."

"I'll help you, Maggie, and I promise I'll do everything I can to make sure you don't get hurt. But if anything does happen, I'm a trained paramedic.

You just have to trust me and try to stay calm. Can you do that?"

"It's me that I don't trust."

"You just need confidence." He put his hat back on. "Let's table your lesson until tomorrow. I can always lend a hand at the corral."

"No." She shook her head. She didn't know what had happened, but somehow this sweet, concerned cowboy had helped her to talk about it. Maybe she'd been misreading him. Maybe he wasn't just concerned about his program's success. In his own way, he led her to some kind of breakthrough. "If you don't mind, I'd like to try my lesson again. Let's do it now. I don't want to think about it overnight, and I don't want to get too far behind the rest."

"You sure?"

"Yes," she said with all the confidence she could muster.

"Excellent decision. Let's go."

Somehow Joe had known if he suggested that they wait on the lesson, Maggie would opt to try again.

A warm feeling settled over him. He wished he could lead her away from here. They could ride in the lower pasture where the wildflowers were in bloom. Hearing her open up—finally—made him want to become even closer to her....

But he couldn't. And before he did something

he'd regret, he'd better stop thinking about Maggie as a woman, and remember that she was just a participant in his program.

They came to the barn door, and Joe could sense her nervousness, hear her breathing quicken. He took her hand in his, and felt the warmth of her skin. He told himself that he was just trying to encourage her, but it felt so good to touch her.

"I'm going to have you bridle and saddle Lady a few times just to get you more comfortable being around her. I'll be right next to you. Ready?"

She nodded. "Ready."

He didn't let go of her hand. Unfortunately, two of the kids and one of the cowboys were in the barn, and they had to suffer through three pairs of raised eyebrows and three sets of eyes looking at their clasped hands.

One pair of eyes belonged to Brandon Avery, Danny's new friend. Maggie's grip tensed, and he wondered if he should drop her hand.

But one scathing look from Joe and the three looked away. He dropped her hand to lead Lady out of her stall, and hooked up the lead rope to a cast-iron circle on the wall. He handed Maggie the horse's bridle and a sugar cube.

"Just remember what I showed you. She'll take the bit. She knows what's happening."

Maggie turned to the horse, and fed her the sugar cube. She'd clearly gotten the hang of things during their morning session, because she didn't need much instruction for the bit, nor for the saddle.

Joe unhooked the lead rope, and handed her the reins. She took them without flinching, though he could see the tension in the set of her shoulders.

"Now lead her outside. I'm right here, next to you," Joe said. It wasn't a hardship being next to Maggie, catching the scent of her floral shampoo whenever she was near.

"So far, so good. Right?"

"You're doing fine. We're going to take Lady on a walk along the river, just so the two of you can get better acquainted."

"It has turned into a gorgeous day."

Joe hadn't noticed. He'd been busy worrying about the beautiful woman next to him. Shedding his coat, he draped it over a fence post. She handed him Lady's reins and did the same.

They walked along the river, Lady neighing softly behind them.

"If you'll hold her for me, I think I'm ready to get on now, Joe."

"Okay, but let me help you." He gave her instructions, and Maggie repeated them. After a few hops, she was sitting in the saddle, looking surprised— and proud of herself.

"There will be no jumping or running. We'll let Lady walk for a while, then we'll call it a day."

When he looked back at Maggie, she was sitting

tall in the saddle and seemed to be enjoying the ride. Every now and then, she'd pet Lady or whisper something to the horse that he couldn't hear.

"I can't believe I'm saying this, but I'm having a great time." She chuckled. "I'm back on a horse after—" She put her hand over her mouth so the next word was muffled, then she removed it. "Years."

He laughed. It seemed like he was always laughing with Maggie.

Ideally, he would have liked it if she took the reins, but he felt that Maggie had made a ton of progress, and he admired her grit.

"Joe, tell me more about the woman you were engaged to. Why didn't you get married?"

"What do you want to know?"

"Well, you know a lot about me, but I don't know anything about you."

He shrugged. "There's not much to tell. Her name was Ellen Rogers. She left me to live in Los Angeles. She said that she didn't want to live on a ranch or in a small town like Mountain Springs."

"I'm sorry. That must have hurt."

"There's nothing to be sorry about. I'm glad I found out sooner than later. She wanted a different lifestyle, and my ranch couldn't compare."

"There's a lot of opportunities in big cities. There's not much around here."

"Not if you don't like ranching or farming," he said, a little defensive.

"I know. I grew up on a dairy farm, remember? But I wasn't home much. From about the age of ten, I was busy taking voice and dancing lessons in Syracuse. Liz got stuck with doing most of my chores, but she loved the farm."

"*You'd* never leave Manhattan for a place like Mountain Springs." It wasn't a question; it was a statement. He just wanted to prove his point.

She shrugged. "I haven't seen much of Mountain Springs yet, but it sure is beautiful here." She gestured to the distant mountains and conifer trees. "Just beautiful. It's not like home at all."

Maggie stared into the distance. She was probably thinking that she'd love to take the first plane out of here. A woman like Maggie didn't belong here any more than she belonged on a dairy farm.

He'd proved his point. Maggie was just like Ellen Rogers.

That was another good reason—maybe the best reason—to stay away from her.

Chapter Six

Later that evening, as everyone roasted marshmallows over the campfire, Maggie kept up a steady supply of graham crackers and squares of chocolate for s'mores.

She thought about how much Joe had helped her this afternoon and she was gaining confidence. Maybe this program had already helped her more than she'd thought possible. Maybe soon she'd even be able to make a decision about something that she'd been worrying over for far too long—quitting the stage.

She stole a glance at Danny. He was still sulking, probably because he'd heard about Joe and her holding hands earlier. It wasn't private enough here to talk to him, and if she called him away from the others, he wouldn't like that either.

She'd just have to wait for the right time.

Tim, the math instructor-turned-rodeo rider, picked up his guitar and started strumming "Red River Valley" and a couple of the cowboys joined in. She joined in, too, once she knew the words. It felt good to sing again.

When the song was over, the kids and cowboys clapped and cheered. She flushed with pleasure just as Joe caught her eye.

Tim started another song, one she didn't know, as Joe took a seat beside her. "I love listening to you sing. We all can see why you're a Broadway star."

She smiled. It was always nice to hear that, especially when it came from the heart.

"With talent like yours, you'll find another show."

She was quiet for a while, then shrugged. "Maybe. Maybe not. I had momentum going, but momentum can be fleeting. But that's all right. It'll be worth it if being here helps Danny in the end."

It surprised Maggie that she was able to vocalize what she'd been thinking about more and more—did she have anything more to accomplish on the stage? She'd already won a Tony, what more was there?

She'd always liked performing, after she got over her initial moments of stage fright. Thankfully, that disappeared when the curtain went up. But for some reason, lately the work itself wasn't as rewarding as before.

She took a sip of water. "All the time I spend in rehearsals and performing has taken a toll on my relationship with Danny."

She often thought that she might like to teach dance and voice. She'd taught at workshops before, and she loved it. She loved how much energy the kids had and how eager they were to learn. But she had to take care of Danny, and teaching was nowhere near as lucrative as performing.

Joe leaned over and rested his arms on his thighs. "You'll figure out how to solve your problem with Danny. Things will get better."

"Promise?"

"I promise." Joe met her gaze, and the firelight made his features look chiseled, masculine.

She sighed. "I just wish I'd been able to put Danny's needs first when Liz died. But I was so caught up in my own misery... I had friends to confide in, to support me, and Danny had no one. I've neglected him miserably. Now I need to make that up." Tears stung her eyes.

"Have you ever apologized to Danny for neglecting him? Explaining how lost *you* were?"

"Why...no. No, I haven't."

"Do you think you should?"

"I should, but I don't know how. I've been avoiding any discussion with him about that time."

"Why?"

"I don't know if I could handle it if he got mad at me, or if it came out that he really hated me for being so neglectful of his needs." She took a deep breath. "I know that kids get mad at their parents all the time, and I don't want to seem clueless about parenting, but this is all new to me. And his getting into trouble is showing me exactly what he thinks of our situation."

"You should give Danny more credit. He's not a bad kid. He just needs to find his way back to a positive direction."

Maggie chuckled. "Don't we all?"

"How about if you talk to him tomorrow? After Danny's school program, you both can go on a picnic for lunch. That'll give you some time away from the group. After that, I'll give you another riding lesson when they are in afternoon school. Sound good?"

"Sounds perfect."

"Well, back to work." Joe stood and pulled a piece of paper from his back pocket. "Can I have everyone's attention, please?" He waited until there was silence. "I have the duty roster for tomorrow. Dan Turner, you'll be picking up litter along the Silver River. See Cookie for a box lunch. Maggie McIntyre, you're assigned to the same cleanup. And

McIntyre, you're also assigned to assist Cookie tomorrow for breakfast."

She felt a warmth inside her grow. Joe Watley obviously knew how to avoid the ribbing Danny would have taken if he'd announced instead that Danny was going on a picnic lunch with his aunt.

Impressive.

Someone would figure it out, she was sure, but at least now they'd have a reason to spend some time together.

She hoped that it would turn out well—for both of them.

Maggie enjoyed working with Cookie, and even talked the cantankerous cowboy into letting her fry the eggs, pancakes and potatoes instead of just shuttling platters to the tables. She was even successful in nudging him into serving a fruit salad to balance some of the grease.

But he wouldn't let her make the coffee.

"It has to be strong enough to float a horseshoe," he'd told her.

After clearing up breakfast, she helped start lunch while the kids went to their morning classes. She also made two picnic lunches—one for herself, and one for Danny.

Armed with their lunch and two big plastic garbage bags to pick up litter, she met Danny by the corral.

They started to walk along the Silver River, and it was clear that Danny wasn't in the mood to talk.

"So, how's everything going so far?" she asked.

"Okay."

"Are you getting along with the other boys?"

"What's that supposed to mean?" He avoided her eyes.

"Just what I asked. Everyone getting along?" she pressed.

"I guess so."

"How about Joe? I think he's doing a great job."

"Brandon Avery told me that you were holding hands with him. I think you like him—a lot."

She took a deep breath and jumped right in. "Look, Danny, I do like Joe, but it's not like that. He's dedicated to making his program work, and I think he really cares about everyone in Cowboy Quest, but that's about it."

Danny shrugged. "Everyone's talking about you two."

"Let them talk. Maybe they don't have anything better to do."

"You just don't get it, do you?" His voice was raised, and Maggie looked at him sharply.

"No, I don't. Talk to me."

"Nothing. Forget it."

Maggie rubbed Danny's shoulder, and to her surprise, he didn't pull away.

"Danny, I'm trying to figure out where we went wrong. I think I know. I neglected you when your mom died. And I'm so very sorry about that."

He appeared to be listening, so she continued.

"I have no excuse other than the fact that I was hurting. My heart was breaking. I loved your mother so much. And she trusted me with raising you and that scared me. It still does. And I'm not doing a good job, Danny. I know that now."

"Forget it," he muttered. "I'm okay."

"But you're not okay, honey. Your not being okay is what got you arrested."

"But—" Danny fell silent, then added, "But why are you scared?"

"Raising a child is a big responsibility. I might not have done everything right at the beginning, but I'm learning from my mistakes."

"I made mistakes, too. I shouldn't have hung out with those kids."

She nodded. "Now you know never to hang around with anyone who'll get you into trouble. Right?"

He nodded.

"And you'll be careful here, too. Right?"

Another nod.

"Danny, you know I have to work. The theater

is all I know, and it's a big time-suck. I'd rather be home with you, but I need to support us."

"I know."

"And you need to stay out of trouble and do better in school."

He shrugged, but didn't say any more, so she thought she'd lighten the conversation. She held her pole in the air. "So I guess we've got to pick up litter. Charge!"

To her surprise, a smile teased the corners of Danny's lips. "Charge," he said under his breath, and they slowly walked the bank of the sparkling river searching for litter until they came to a bench, then they sat down.

"Tell me, what do you like about the ranch so far? There must be something," Maggie said. "Talk to me like we used to when your mom was alive."

"I like my horse. His name is Thunderbolt," he finally said.

"What color is he?" she asked, trying anything to get him to talk.

"He's like a reddish brown. He's a quarterhorse, and Joe said that if I make enough progress on my lesson, I'd be able to trot him, then gallop."

Maggie hadn't seen her nephew so visibly excited in a long time. Usually she had to check his pulse for signs of life.

Before they left for the dreaded cattle drive, she'd probably have to learn to trot and gallop, too. Her throat sudden went dry, and she was glad that she packed some iced tea.

"Joe said that a cowboy must be gentle with children, the elderly and animals. He said that includes taking care of my horse and brushing, watering and feeding him and not doing anything to hurt him."

"Taking care of an animal is a big responsibility," she said, thrilled at Danny's enthusiasm. Then it hit her. Danny had never had a pet or anything to be responsible for. She never could see getting a cat or a dog, since no one was usually home, for the most part. "I think that a horse has to be one of the biggest. I'm glad that you're listening to Joe."

"Some of the kids aren't listening to him. They think that the program is lame, especially Brandon." He lowered his voice. "But I kinda like it. And I freaking can't wait for the cattle drive."

"Daniel Anthony Turner, did I hear you right? You like Cowboy Quest?" She was just about to ruffle his hair when he laughed and ducked.

"Naw. I didn't say that." He grinned, opening the bag that contained his picnic lunch.

They laughed and for a moment she saw a hint of the carefree child he'd been—when Liz was healthy. That was the Danny that she'd wanted back permanently. Happy for this all-too-rare moment of closeness, Maggie pulled her nephew's slight frame to her and wrapped her arms around him. She felt some weight dissolve from her shoulders. This talk was the first step in clearing the air with Danny, and she made a mental note to thank Joe for giving her the opportunity to spend some quality time with him.

She'd made a lot of progress with Danny this morning, and obviously so had Joe, since Danny was quoting him.

Was she wrong to have doubted the big, strong cowboy?

It was one o'clock and time for Maggie's lesson. Joe waved as she walked up the hill toward him, smiling.

Either she was looking forward to her lesson, or things went well with Danny. He hoped for both.

She was a little breathless when she finally reached him.

"Have a good time picking up litter?"

"The best." Her eyes sparkled. "I had a good talk with Danny. Finally."

Thank goodness. "That was the plan. I'll arrange something like that again."

"That'd be great, Joe. Danny seems like he's really enjoying the program so far. He's even quoting you."

"No kidding?"

"No kidding," she said. "You're reaching him."

"Oh, I think you are, too." Maggie deserved the credit more than he did. She was the one who put her emotions on the line. "Now, how about your lesson? Are you ready to ride Lady by yourself? I thought we'd take the horses to the high pasture."

"I'm as ready as I'll ever be."

As he got his own horse, Checkmate, ready, he watched Maggie bridle and saddle Lady. He could see her biting her lip, thinking about every move she was making. Lady was patient, even helping her along, taking the bit perfectly.

"Ready to mount up?"

He held the reins for her. After a few hops, she was in the saddle. He handed her the reins, and she looked at them as if he was handing her a tarantula. "Maggie?"

"I can do this."

"You certainly can."

"I'm not even breathing hard."

"I don't think you're breathing at all." He raised an eyebrow. "Are you?"

"No."

He bit back a grin. "Relax. We'll have a good time. Okay?"

She finally took the reins. "Okay."

Her whole face glowed when she smiled, her eyes shone like twin emeralds and her perfect lips showcased white teeth. He liked the way her blond hair swirled around her face in the breeze.

Sure, she was beautiful. But most of all he admired her courage in getting on a horse in spite of her fears. And it took a lot of courage to corner Danny about the rift that had come between them for a long time.

"When you're ready, Maggie. Lift the reins, squeeze her sides gently with your knees and just say 'walk.' She'll know what you want. And if you want her to stop, just say 'whoa.' The Cowboy Quest horses are voice trained."

"That's easy enough." She nodded. "Walk."

Lady did as instructed, and Maggie looked surprised. Joe followed on Checkmate. When the pathway opened up, he moved next to her.

"Relax your shoulders, Maggie. I just want you to get comfortable sitting on Lady."

Joe could tell that Checkmate wanted to run. The horse was too frisky and needed exercise. They'd had too much rain last week, which pushed the exercise schedule back. Because Checkmate was a runner, Joe and the other seasoned cowboys were the only ones who were allowed to ride him. He wasn't qualified as a Cowboy Quest horse yet, but maybe later he'd take the horse out for a long gallop through the upper meadow.

"Remember to keep your heels down, Maggie. You're doing great."

They made small talk—the weather (unusually warm for spring), the scenery (fabulous), her talk with Danny (long overdue), and the cattle drive in two days (she was dreading it).

"The cattle drive will be fun, too," he said. In fact, he couldn't wait to get started. At least his time would be spread out among all the participants and he wouldn't have to spend as much time with Maggie. He was with her too much—and he was enjoying her too much.

She was a beautiful distraction, but she was still a distraction, and he needed to concentrate on Cowboy Quest. He had to be on the lookout for trouble so he could squelch it before it happened.

He pulled on the horse's reins to hold him in check. He was high spirited today.

"Do you think that I'll be a good enough rider for the cattle drive?" Maggie asked.

"You'll be fine. So will the others. You can walk Lady all the way through it and follow alongside Cookie's chuck wagon. It's a real roundup, you know. We're moving the cattle from the winter pasture to the summer pasture."

"How long will it take?"

"We'll be five days and four nights on the trail, depending on the weather. To tell you the truth, my crew and I could do it in an overnight, but we extend it for Cowboy Quest. Some of the participants have never camped before. Can you believe that?"

She put her hand over her heart and faked a heart attack. "No! Some people have never camped before? What's wrong with them? Aliens? Or do they just prefer four-star hotels and indoor toilets like I do instead of sleeping on the ground and carrying a shovel?"

He turned around in the saddle, ready to dazzle her with a witty retort when Checkmate whinnied and pawed the ground.

Maggie let out a blood-curdling scream. "Snake!"

Out of the corner of his eye, he saw a snake curled up and ready to strike. He yanked his knife from the leather sheath at his side, and threw it.

As he leaned over to see if he'd hit his mark, his sudden motion unsettled Checkmate, who bucked, side-stepped, then reared.

Off balance, Joe flew through the air and landed flat on his back. Checkmate took off at a dead run.

Maggie screamed again as Lady took off at a gallop, chasing Checkmate!

Chapter Seven

Joe dragged himself up from the ground. Being tossed was a rookie mistake. He'd never been caught off guard or off balance like that before.

Damn snake.

He scrambled to his feet and saw Checkmate and Lady galloping away, with Maggie hanging on for dear life.

He whistled. *Short, long, short.* The two horses immediately slowed down, then stopped completely. Another whistle brought them walking back to him.

He brushed himself off and picked up his hat, grabbed his knife and returned it to the case on his hip. Then he hurried to meet the horses—and Maggie—so they wouldn't have to encounter what was left of the snake.

"Whoa," he said as he approached them. The horses immediately stopped. He looked up at Maggie. "Are you okay?"

Her eyes were shiny, her cheeks were pink—with fear or excitement? He couldn't tell.

"I—I'm okay. Just a little rattled, pardon the pun." She shuddered. "What the hell happened?"

He shook his head. "I'm really sorry, Maggie. Even the best-trained horse can't be taught to stay calm with a snake present."

"Did you get the snake?"

Joe nodded. "Yeah, he's history. But I'm pretty embarrassed. I haven't been tossed by a horse in years."

I was too busy looking at you to pay attention to anything else.

"Don't be embarrassed on my account." She put her index finger over her lip. "I won't tell a soul."

The twinkle in her eyes told him that it would be all over the ranch in less than an hour.

"Yeah, sure." He chuckled. "Shall we go back?"

"Don't go back on my account. My confidence level just skyrocketed. I stayed on!"

He swung onto Checkmate's back. "You sure

did. That was pretty outstanding riding for a city slicker."

If she could ride like that, she could handle anything that might come her way.

Maggie couldn't stop grinning at Joe's compliment. Her ride hadn't been pretty by anyone's standards, and she'd been petrified that she'd be thrown, but she'd managed to stick with Lady.

She had never been so glad to hear a whistle in her life.

"I forgot to say 'whoa,'" she admitted now. "But I heard you whistle."

"As a safety measure, I also trained them to stop on a certain whistle command. Then two short whistles will get them back to you. All the Cowboy Quest horses go through vigorous training and testing." He petted Checkmate's neck. "This guy here is a little too frisky yet, but he'll come along in time."

"So what's on the schedule later this afternoon?" she asked. "I think I just had my galloping lesson."

"Roping."

She felt a warm rush of confidence. She could do that. No problem.

"Bring it on."

He gestured to the gathering of the others by

the corral, where the roping lesson was about to begin.

Joe waved his hand to one of the cowboys. "Would you mind taking care of our horses so we can join the others?"

"No problem, boss."

Joe gave him a slap on the back in gratitude, and motioned for her to walk ahead of him. Maggie waited for the usual snickers from the participants and eye-rolling from Danny, but they were mesmerized, watching as Ronnie twirled a rope overhead, brought it down to foot level, then stepped over it. Back and forth Ronnie stepped, moving the rope in figure eights.

"That looks as easy as pie," Maggie whispered to Joe. At least she thought she whispered. As the group laughed at her statement, Ronnie handed her the rope.

He smiled at her as if they shared a secret.

Joe took the rope out of her hands. "Ronnie… uh…I don't think that Maggie—"

Maggie took the rope back. "Hang on." She stepped forward to give herself some more room. "I may be a city slicker, but I'll give it a try."

She tried to remember what she'd learned from Baxter Bello, a trick rope expert who was hired to teach her when she starred in *Annie Get Your Gun*. He'd called it the Texas Skip.

She'd played Annie Oakley six years ago, and

she was certainly rusty in the roping department, but she wanted to impress Joe. She got a feel for the rope, letting out a little at a time from the knot, as she slowly began to spin it. Baxter's voice rang in her ear, "Go slow. Don't rush. It's all in the wrist."

She concentrated, knowing that if she could pull off a couple of jumps, the kids and cowboys would be dazzled. Glancing at the astonishment on their faces, she saw they were already impressed that she'd gotten this far.

Now!

She jumped over the loop, again and again. When a loud whoop went up from the crowd, she lost her focus and the rope wrapped around her body.

She got a round of applause from everyone, and she took a bow. Catching Danny's eye, she saw a glimmer of admiration, and pride shot through her. Even his new friend Brandon looked impressed.

But Joe looked the most surprised, and heat pooled in her belly as he looked her over.

She spotted Ronnie, grinning from ear to ear.

"How did you know?" she asked him.

"I saw you in *Annie Get Your Gun*. Your trick roping was great, so I got a video and taught myself."

Maggie handed the rope back to him. "What brought you to New York City?"

"A wedding." Ronnie looked around at the group. "My mother wanted to see you in *Annie* so I took her."

Joe clapped his hands once. "For the rest of us who can't do Maggie and Ronnie's trick, we are going to stick with the basics. Break down into teams of three, please."

They kicked up some dust, shuffling around until they stood in groups of one cowboy, two participants and one plastic cow head stuck into a hay bale per team.

Danny quickly fell into step with Brandon with Quint as their staff member. She couldn't understand why Danny gravitated to Brandon, especially since he admitted that Brandon didn't like Cowboy Quest. Danny seemed to like it a little more than before. Even if Danny liked Cowboy Quest a lot, he would still act apathetic to his pals.

She and Joe were with Rick, one of the more sullen boys. He was a shorter, muscular boy with tattoos all over his body, including some homemade ones on his neck.

"I'm sure you've all seen old Westerns," Joe said, twirling a rope over his head. "The rope is used to keep the cattle moving, and to get strays out of ditches and the like. They aren't too smart, so they get in all kinds of jams. You have each been given one rope. It's yours while you are here. Take care of your rope and don't lose it. It should be tied to your saddle when you're riding. When you're not riding, practice with it."

Maggie did as Joe instructed and let her rope

soar at the horns on the plastic cow. Perfect shot! Roping was a piece of cake. Rick was struggling, so Joe spent more time with him. They roped from different angles and distances from the cow head, but she always hit her mark.

As she waited for Rick, she couldn't help but overhear Quint with Danny and Brandon. "C'mon, boys, you're not even trying. Now pay attention and stop talking like a couple of old hens."

She was just about to say something to Danny when she remembered how Joe had asked her nicely to butt out, that the cowboy staff would take care of discipline.

Danny halfheartedly roped the cow head, and he didn't do badly, hitting the mark more often than not. She could tell he cared, that he wanted to do well, but he wouldn't show it. It appeared to her that Brandon was acting like he couldn't care less, and Danny was simply going along with him.

"That's it for today," Joe said. "Tomorrow you'll all get a chance to try roping a calf or two on horseback. Therefore, I suggest that you practice tonight after your homework."

Just then the dinner bell rang. Maggie walked to the bunkhouse with the rest of the group, trying specifically to stay away from Joe so the other boys wouldn't tease Danny.

"He likes you—a lot," Danny had said earlier. *"Everyone knows it."*

Looking at Joe, she couldn't help noticing the confidence in his stance—his muscular thighs, encased in worn denim. But she noticed more than his physical appearance. She admired his patience, the way he never spoke down to the kids, the way he was slowly winning over even the most angry of the lot, with the possible exception of Brandon Avery.

There were many things about Joe that she liked, but what was the sense of flirting, or taking their relationship—such as it was—to the next level? The two of them were from different worlds, and they each had lives from which they couldn't—wouldn't—walk away. Maggie's life was in New York, not in tiny Mountain Springs, Wyoming.

But what was she thinking? She'd never have to make that difficult decision because she wouldn't let her attraction get that far.

As everyone entered the bunkhouse, Maggie turned to walk uphill to the ranch house, desperate to change her dirty clothes when Danny appeared next to her.

"Some day will you show me that rope trick, Aunt Maggie?"

"Sure. Whenever you'd like. How did your roping go?"

"Okay. I did better than a lot of the other guys," he said with pride.

"Good for you!"

Danny looked toward the rest of the group, then

back at her. "Some of the cowboys are going to tell ghost stories at the campfire tonight. Are you going?"

He actually wanted her company? Or maybe he didn't want her to go to the campfire, so he could be alone with his pals.

She chose to believe the former.

"What would a campfire be without ghost stories? I'll be there. I'm just going to change clothes and get a jacket. I'll be down soon."

He nodded, then took off at a dead run to catch up with the others.

This was sure a pleasant change from the sullen and surly boy he'd been for so long. Maybe their earlier conversation by the river had made a difference after all.

Would it have made a difference if they'd had such a talk after Liz died two years ago? She didn't know.

Whatever it was, Danny was coming around, and she couldn't be happier. She just hoped that things would keep getting better....

"Tomorrow is going to be a full day," Joe announced at the campfire. "There will be more riding lessons, another roping practice, and then we'll pack for the cattle drive. The wagons have to be packed with tents, sleeping bags, food and other supplies.

The bunkhouse will be cleaned and swept before we leave at sunrise on Wednesday."

A buzz of excitement traveled around the campfire, and then the boys caught themselves and the eye-rolling and elbow-nudging began again. Danny did smile, albeit briefly.

He might be turning into a regular cowboy after all, Joe thought.

Better yet, Danny was starting not to care about what the other kids thought. He'd overheard him tell Rick that he didn't want a tattoo, no matter how cool everyone thought they were.

He wondered if Maggie noticed that Danny was starting to be his own man.

Maggie. She was always on his mind.

She'd surprised him twice today—by hanging on to Lady and with the rope trick. He just might make a cowgirl out of her yet.

Nah. Maggie was a city gal through and through, he thought regretfully. But even though the lights of Broadway might normally shine on her, right now she looked beautiful by the light of the campfire.

He wondered if he could talk her into singing for them, but he didn't want to single her out—she was just a participant in Cowboy Quest, after all.

Yeah, right.

He watched as she toasted a marshmallow, how she licked her lips after she ate it. He noticed her twinkling eyes and was attuned to her every laugh.

And when she met his gaze, he was rewarded with a smile.

But her face quickly fell when she looked over and saw Danny watching them. He stood up and walked away from the fire, heading for the bunkhouse.

Dammit.

They weren't even doing anything, so why did he feel so guilty?

As the campfire died out, everyone began to shuffle to the bunkhouse.

"Hang on a minute, Maggie," Joe said. "I'll walk you home."

He snapped his fingers. "I have to remind Jake to feed Calico when we're on the trail ride. Actually, I'd like you to meet him. We go way back to grammar school, and we were in the rodeos together for several years."

"What exactly did you and Jake do with the rodeo?"

"We did timed team roping. He was the header, and I was the heeler—he roped the head of a running calf, I roped the heels."

"I've never been to a rodeo."

"Then you don't know what you're missing." He shoveled dirt onto the fire to smother it. "Someday, we'll have to go."

It was as if he was asking her for a date. But that wasn't his intent. Still, he'd like nothing better than to take her to a rodeo, show her Mountain Springs and hit the local honky tonks and dance with her. But would she even go?

"Sounds like fun. I'd love to, Joe."

That was the reply he'd hoped for, but unfortunately, she'd be going home after Cowboy Quest.

Looking up at the vast Wyoming sky dotted with twinkling stars, Maggie felt a pang of sorrow. "I'm missing my sister tonight."

"That's understandable. You loved her, and she loved you—enough to trust you with her only son."

"And I've failed her," she said, regretfully.

"No, you haven't. You're here, aren't you? And Danny's coming around. Right?"

She shrugged. "He does seem to be coming out of his shell a little."

"Excellent. Now don't worry." His deep, calm voice almost made her believe that everything would be all right.

"Are you ready to go?" he asked. "Big day tomorrow."

Maggie turned on her flashlight and started up the path. Even before she left New York, thoughts of the cattle drive were on her mind. She didn't know if she had the pluck to ride a horse all day, camp out at night and keep up with her chores. But if it would keep Danny in her custody, she'd ride a horse to the moon and back.

"It'll be fun, you'll see." Joe put his hand on the small of her back to guide her over an uneven patch of land, and her mouth suddenly went dry.

"The trail is pretty easy and straightforward," he continued. "No surprises. As you already experienced, animals can be unpredictable, but all of my staff will be on high alert at all times. I want everyone back safe and sound."

"I second that."

They reached the front porch, and Maggie suddenly remembered the night before, when Joe seemed like he was about to kiss her. But that must have been her imagination.

As she turned to unlock the door, his calloused hand wrapped around hers. She met his dark, smoky gaze, and her heart skipped a beat.

His lips looked warm and inviting, and they curved up into a sexy grin.

Her common sense was at war with her heart. She liked him—a lot—but that didn't matter. There could be no future for their relationship. Even if they did start something, she didn't want to be hurt down the line. Also, Danny and the rest of the participants were already on high alert waiting to catch them in a compromising situation, and the last thing she wanted was to do more damage to her already fragile nephew.

She dropped his hand, and unlocked the door

before she changed her mind. "Good night, Joe. I'll see you bright and early."

He held her gaze, and she couldn't ignore the heat in his eyes. "I'll see you tomorrow. Sweet dreams, Maggie."

Escaping into the house, she closed the door and leaned on it, willing her pulse to stop racing.

She had a feeling that things weren't going to go exactly as planned.

Chapter Eight

Two days later, Joe stood next to his horse at the flagpole and smiled at the yawning boys standing next to their horses. Maggie was with Lady.

"Hope you're all well rested, because we're about to start our cattle drive. We're going to move the Silver River cattle from their lower winter grounds to their higher summer grounds. We'll brand those that need to be branded and separate any Gold Buckle Ranch cattle that got mixed in and drive them to Jake Dixon's summer pasture."

Quint had advised him about the high level of excitement in the bunkhouse last night. Even a couple of their least responsive boys were showing signs of life. Joe wanted to keep that excitement going.

Danny looked like he was about ready to jump out of his skin. So did Maggie, though he suspected for different reasons.

Maggie. He'd wanted to kiss her the other night.

After watching her at the campfire, seeing how the moonlight and the firelight played across her face, he'd longed to feel her lips against his.

She'd been the strong one before, the one who'd terminated whatever was happening between them, and brought him back to reality.

She was probably worried about what Danny would think.

As they all gathered and prepared to leave, Joe surveyed his crew. Cookie was at the one o'clock position, perched on his authentic chuck wagon with a team of horses. It was packed with provisions, first aid kits, water and extra gear.

A covered wagon sat at three o'clock, loaded with sleeping bags, tents, rain gear and other supplies. Quint sat in the so-called driver's seat, holding the reins.

Ronnie was the wrangler in charge of the remuda. He'd see that the horses were taken care of, along with their tack, food and water. Everyone would look after his or her own horse, but Ronnie would supervise overall.

Joe stole a look at Maggie. She looked just like a cowgirl in her white hat. She was listening attentively to instructions from the various team leaders, while maintaining a steady grip on Lady's reins.

Everyone was fed, the horses were saddled and everything was loaded. It was time to go.

Ronnie gave Joe the thumbs-up sign.

"Westward ho!" Joe yelled, pumping the air with his fist.

"Westward ho!" yelled the crowd, pumping the air in return. Though some of the boys snickered as if they'd just done the stupidest thing, their excitement was palpable, whether they wanted to admit it or not.

Joe looked at Maggie. Her cheeks were pink, and she seemed ready for the challenge of a forty-mile round-trip cattle drive. He'd plotted out the easiest route possible for Cowboy Quest beginners, complete with swimming holes and some of the best scenery that Wyoming had to offer.

Maggie mounted her horse with only a couple of hops, and he rode up to her on Checkmate. "You sure you're ready?" he asked.

She smiled. "I'm as ready as I'll ever be. And I think Danny's raring to go. I've never seen him this excited!"

Joe laughed. "Good. I want to keep the excitement up and keep them busy. Then they won't even have time to think about getting into trouble."

He slapped his thigh. "Well, let's rock and roll.

I'm going to ask Danny if he'd like to ride in the lead with me. Ronnie will ride next to you. Tell him if you need anything."

"Got it." She hesitated—obviously she wanted to say something. He waited. "Joe?"

"Yeah?"

"I just want you to know that I appreciate everything you've done. You're a great...um..."

"Trail boss?"

She laughed. "Yeah. A great trail boss."

He glanced down at her butt. "Thanks, but you might be singing a different tune after a day in the saddle."

Joe was wrong. Maggie was singing the blues after just seventy-four minutes in the saddle; she couldn't imagine what a whole day would be like. She was using muscles that she didn't even know she had.

Thank goodness someone called for a break. It was a relief to be able to stretch her legs. She waved to Danny, and he slowly walked to where she was standing.

"What do you think, Danny? Pretty cool?"

"It's cool." His words were blandly delivered, but his eyes sparkled.

"I'm glad you're having a good time."

"Joe picked me first to lead the way with him!"

"I know. Another cool thing, huh?" Maggie

asked, careful not to say or do something that would clam him up.

"Danny, come over here," Brandon called.

Danny turned to walk away from her, but Maggie put her hand on the boy's shoulder. "Danny, you don't have to do what he says. We were having a nice conversation, and—"

He moved away from her grip. "I gotta go."

She sighed. They'd been sharing a great moment, at least until Brandon called him over.

If only Danny would stick up for himself. If only he'd realize that he didn't have to be a follower, but that he had a mind of his own—a *good* mind.

If only she knew how to reach him....

Looking up, she noticed Joe walking over to the huddle of boys, and she wondered if he caught that little scene between Danny and her.

"Any problems, cowboys? Any questions I can answer?" he asked.

"Yeah, where's the nearest mall?" one of the boys joked.

"Over in Casper. If you get walking, you could make it there in a couple of weeks." Joe laughed. "Time to mount up. Anyone want to take a turn leading the way?"

More silence. Joe turned to Danny, "Dan, looks like you get to go again. How about it?"

He shrugged his shoulders. "I guess so."

They walked their horses for two more miles,

following the Silver River. Maggie enjoyed the scenery—the vast blue sky dotted with cotton candy clouds, and the green grass peppered with wildflowers, their colorful heads bowing to the breeze. She noticed spots of the river where the current rushed and spun almost like a whirlpool, and she longed to sit right in the middle of the water and soothe her aching muscles.

Joe was talking to Ronnie, who rode on his right, and Danny was listening to his friends, who had caught up with him. All around her, the cowboys and kids kept up an easy banter, with the possible exception of Brandon, Rick and Danny. Brandon's scowl was becoming more pronounced as time went by, and Maggie noticed that most of the kids were giving them all a wide berth. Danny was nodding his head, looking as if he was agreeing with whatever Brandon said.

Why can't Danny stand on his own?

Lunch consisted of hot dogs and beans and handfuls of potato chips and big McIntosh apples. Cookie fried the hot dogs in a big cast-iron pan as Maggie stirred the beans that she'd placed in two Dutch ovens set on the propane camp stoves they'd hauled in the chuck wagon.

In between stirring, she set out the utensils, metal plates and paper napkins on the back of the wagon. Everyone could help themselves when they were ready.

Maggie made up a plate for herself and went to eat in the shade of a maple tree. The leaves were a brilliant shade of green, and the air smelled fresh, clean—so different from the exhaust-filled air back home. Her butt and legs were killing her after four hours in the saddle, and she couldn't imagine what she would feel like in the morning.

Suddenly, Danny walked over to her, carrying his plate.

"Hey, Danny. What's up?"

"Just thought I'd sit with you for a minute."

He flopped down on a patch of ground next to her, watching the action.

They ate in strained silence until Brandon and Rick sat down nearby and began looking over at them.

"What's that about?" she asked Danny. "Why the laughing and the faces at us?"

"They're just fooling around." He shrugged, obviously trying to play it down.

"They don't seem to like anything, but I know that you liked leading the wagon train with Joe. I'm sure you got teased about that."

"Yeah." Another shrug.

"Come on, Danny. No one's listening, it's just you and me. Would it kill you to admit that you're having a great time?"

"So you can remind me that I should be glad that I'm not in an institution?"

The hurt in his tone stunned her for a moment, and she struggled to find her voice. "Daniel Turner, I wasn't going to say that at all. I just hoped we could have a few minutes together like we had the other day while we were picking up litter."

"Oh, please. That was just a bogus job made up by Joe so we could talk."

"Who said that?"

Silence.

She tried again. "So what if it was a bogus job? We did talk, and I think it was good for us. What happened between then and now?"

Danny pulled up a clump of grass and shot it in front of him. "Nothing. Nothing's happened. Why do you say that?"

She'd bet a paycheck that something was up. He was too defensive, too secretive, even for him.

He scrambled to his feet. "Anything else?"

"No. Go back to your friends. Sorry that I bothered you." She couldn't keep the sarcasm out of her voice. Two steps forward, ten gallops back.

Disheartened, Maggie got up and went to the chuck wagon to help with the dishes.

Cookie had put big pots of water on to boil. The dishes would be washed, dried and packed for the next leg of the ride. Cookie had explained that they didn't use plastic or paper plates on the trail so they'd keep their trash to a minimum. Whatever trash was left, they'd bring back to the Silver Ranch and dispose of it properly.

But she wasn't needed to do the dishes. Two of the boys were assigned to that chore.

She walked over to where Joe stood with Ronnie. She wanted to let Joe know that something seemed to be going on with the boys, but she didn't have any hard facts or solid evidence—just a hunch.

Besides, she had to admit that Joe could read the signs of upcoming trouble just as well as or better than she could.

She was going to butt out. She ought to give Joe more credit for knowing what was happening in his own program. "Um...I just wanted to know if there's anything else I can do to help."

"Nothing, but thanks," said Joe. "Just get ready to go. We'll leave in ten minutes."

"Okay. See you both later."

As she turned, she noticed all the boys staring in her direction, shooting daggers at her. They thought she was a snitch—which was ridiculous since she didn't have any specific information.

But *something* was up, and her nephew was in the thick of it.

Her stomach roiled. Didn't he get it? Didn't he know what was at stake?

Chapter Nine

Joe popped the snaps of his cuffs and rolled up the sleeves of his shirt. If ever he hated a job, it was putting together a tent. Right now, it looked like orange-and-yellow roadkill.

Looking over at Maggie's space right next to his, he noticed that her tent was lopsided. A slight breeze would render it uninhabitable. She'd obviously missed a step in the directions.

She held the directions close to her face, mumbling to herself. "I can do this. I can do this."

The boys were busy putting up their tents, too. They were sleeping four to a tent, plus a cowboy with them to chaperone. He assigned them carefully, trying to break up some of the cliques that had already formed. At least they were working together as teams, helping each other, figuring out the directions.

But Maggie was alone, and she'd have to bunk alone. Joe had purposely picked a spot near hers, just in case she needed something. Cougars and bears, along with other potentially dangerous wildlife, roamed here.

Who was he kidding? He just wanted to be near her.

He touched the gun that he carried concealed on his side and felt for the bowie knife that hung from his belt buckle. Both were the cowboy's best friends when in a jam, and nothing was going to happen to the thirteen people who were in his charge.

He looked over at Maggie and realized that he was *always* looking at Maggie. When she wasn't nearby, he'd look for her to appear. Somehow, in the short time he'd known her, she always made his day brighter.

Her tent looked much better now. Maybe he ought to offer her a bribe to put up his!

But he didn't have to. She walked toward him, smiling, her hips swaying, her hair blowing in the breeze. He could look at her long legs all day, every day.

"Need help, Joe?"

"Sure." He didn't, but he wanted to be with her. "Would you put that center pole together for me?"

"I'd be delighted."

She bent over to pick up the poles, and her jeans pulled taut over her backside. He let out a puff of air, and forced himself to concentrate on laying the nylon flat on the ground.

When she handed him the pole, his hand closed over hers. She jumped slightly.

Had she noticed the spark between them, too?

She diverted her eyes from his and went back to the pile of poles. "I'll connect the rest," she said, bending over again.

He wanted to make love to her.

The thought rushed into his consciousness and caught him unawares.

But it was true. He wanted to make love to Maggie, but he couldn't. He wasn't the type to have casual flings and walk away. When he made love to a woman, it meant something.

He thought it had meant something with Ellen, but apparently she hadn't felt the same. She'd hurt him…badly. And just when he thought he'd recovered from her betrayal, in walked Maggie McIntyre, Broadway star and guardian of one of the boys in Cowboy Quest.

So a relationship between them—physical or otherwise—wouldn't work. No way.

It had to be business only. No more fantasies,

no more seeking her out, no more sitting by her or walking with her.

Could he do it?

What was with Joe, Maggie wondered as she helped Cookie serve sloppy joes and a big salad. She thought they were going to sit together for supper, but he'd left her in his dust, muttering some excuse about going over the duty roster for tomorrow.

She'd got the impression that he was only being partially honest with her.

Thinking back, he started acting strange when she'd volunteered to help him with his tent. Very strange.

And he'd abandoned the tent project just as soon as they'd started. What was so hard about sliding his main pole into the smooth opening?

Oh!

She felt her cheeks flame. Oh, no! How could she have been so stupid?

And what was with the writers who made up the tent assembly instructions? Was that their idea of a joke?

She chuckled. Then she outright laughed. Then she doubled over. If anyone was watching her, they would think something was wrong with her.

Poor Joe, she thought.

She had to apologize to him and explain that she had just been oblivious to the entire thing.

Had it been that long for her that she didn't even realize what she'd been reading?

Yes. It had been a long time—three years, to be exact—and it had been Jean-Paul Gordon, an actor she'd met in rehearsal. Jean-Paul had been climbing the ladder to success, and he thought that he could get fame and publicity by sleeping with her. They were linked in the New York gossip columns, but the news never reached Los Angeles, which was Jean-Paul's goal. He eschewed the old adage that any kind of publicity was better than no publicity at all.

He'd hurt her deeply, and as time went by, she'd healed. But his betrayal made her more cautious, more guarded and less willing to trust her heart.

She was already enamored with Joe Watley, and it wouldn't take much for her to succumb to the sexy cowboy. But she had Danny to think of—she didn't want him to think that she was rejecting him for Joe or anyone else. Besides, she wasn't the type to have a fling…or was that just what she needed?

Maybe Joe was the guy to have a fling with. But the timing was certainly off.

There would never be a good time—not when she was in Cowboy Quest, with Danny and everyone else watching their every move.

She stole a glance at Joe. With his formfitting jeans she could see his hard thighs, his taut butt and how his tooled leather belt cinched his trim waist.

He always wore a big, gold oval belt buckle, a trophy from his rodeo days.

He looked rough and rugged and...hot.

The dishes were done and put away, and she noticed everyone gathered at the nightly campfire. She walked over to join the group. A short, nervous kid with wire-rimmed glasses—Troy, she thought— picked up a lawn chair from a stack, opened it and gestured for her to sit down.

"Thanks, Troy."

Troy wasn't one of the guys that Danny hung out with, but Maggie wished he would—he seemed to be a nice, thoughtful kid. She wondered what had happened to bring him to Cowboy Quest, but didn't ask. If they wanted to share something about their past, fine. Otherwise, she kept her conversations with the other boys light.

She accepted a marshmallow on a stick and put it over the fire. Before it finished toasting, she felt a fat raindrop hit her head, and heard more sizzle in the fire as the skies opened.

"Everyone to their tents. This rain is going to be heavy," yelled Quint.

By the time she made it to her tent, she was soaked clear through. Turning on the battery-powered lantern, she decided to change and get out of her wet clothes.

Joe ducked into his tent for his rain slicker and plastic cover for his hat. He'd make the rounds to see if everyone was okay, but as soon as he stepped out of his tent, he froze.

Mesmerized, he watched as Maggie—or rather the silhouette of Maggie—took her bra off. He could even make out the curve of her breasts and the peaks of her nipples when she moved.

Lifting up her hair, she stretched, then hung her bra over a pole in the middle of the tent.

He really should stop watching—and at least warn her that she was so visible—but his feet wouldn't move. It was as if some unknown force had glued him to the ground.

She hung her wet shirt over the end of her cot, and was slipping into a dry one.

He *had* to warn her. If anyone else was looking, it would be embarrassing.

Walking to the front of her tent, he said her name as quietly as possible over the roar of the rain. "Maggie."

"Who is it?"

"Joe. I have to talk to you."

"Uh, wait a minute."

He could hear rustling, as if she was pulling on clothes. He could only hope…

"Come in."

He helped her with the zipper on the opening of the tent and entered. Thankfully, she had been assigned a tent that he could stand up in.

"What are you doing here?"

He didn't know how to begin. He noticed her lantern. The two of them would be silhouetted now. Not good.

"I just wanted to tell you that with the lantern, you can see every move you make in here. I saw you undressing…"

"Oh, no! Don't say any more." She turned the knob of the lantern, and they were in complete darkness. "I didn't know. Do you think that any of the kids saw? What about the cowboys?"

"Probably just me. I was going to make my rounds, that's how I noticed." When lightning flashed, he could see her lips, thin with worry, and it struck him that he'd like to kiss them back into a smile. Maggie looked so much younger and freer when she smiled.

She stood facing him. "That was a stupid mistake on my part. I should have realized."

He wished she wouldn't stand so close. He could smell the freshness of the rainwater on her skin, on her hair.

"Well, I'd better get back to my rounds," he finally said.

"It sounds awful out there." She brushed her hair back with a hand. "Are the horses okay?"

"Ronnie has probably checked them already, but I'll double-check."

"Let me go with you."

"That's not necessary. You'll just get wet."

"I don't want to stay in this tent in a storm. I'd rather be...with you."

That was all he needed to hear. He pulled her close to him, and before he could think about it or change his mind, he tasted her lips.

She sighed softly and he took that as a sign that he should continue. Slanting his lips over hers, he felt as if he were falling over a steep cliff with no chance for survival.

Joe Watley sure could kiss.

Maggie kissed him with a hunger she'd never felt before. Heaven help her, she wanted to taste him— and she wanted more.

His lips were warm, sweet, and she wanted him out of the wet rain slicker. She wanted to toss his cowboy hat away so she could run her fingers through his thick, black hair.

"Take it off, Joe," she ordered, tugging on his coat.

"Mmmm..." he said, shrugging his coat off. It landed on the beige nylon floor.

His lips never moved from hers, but he did take his hat off. It landed on top of his coat.

Running her hands over the soft flannel of his shirt, she could feel the hard muscles of his chest and arms. She ran her fingertips over his face, his high cheekbones, the set of his jaw, the arch of his brow.

And she still wanted more. She wanted to see him, all of him. Without his shirt and his snug jeans, belt and big buckle. She wanted to touch every inch of him.

But Joe was taking things slowly—and she was ready to scream.

"More," she said. His hands moved to the hem of her shirt. "Yes. Yes."

Was the cold air puckering her nipples, or was it the heat of his hands?

He ran his calloused fingers over her sides, her stomach and the undersides of her breasts. His thumbs rubbed her nipples until they became even harder. When his warm mouth closed over one, she moaned, a roll of thunder drowning out her voice.

It had been so long. Too long.

He pulled the shirt over her head, and teased her other nipple with his mouth and tongue. It was exquisite torture.

"I want you," Joe said softly. He sucked on her earlobe and she thought she was going to faint right then, right there.

"Yes. Oh, yes."

A crack of lightning illuminated the tent, and she wondered for a moment if their silhouettes could be seen.

They should stop.

But all she cared about right now was the hunk of a cowboy who wanted her, whose lips were tasting her, loving her, making her knees weak and her mouth dry.

The whinny of a horse and another noise outside made them both stop and listen.

"Hey, Joe! Joe, are you in your tent? Joe?"

Danny.

It was as if someone had thrown a cold bucket of rain on them both. Joe quickly buttoned his shirt and slipped back into his coat and hat. Maggie tugged her sweatshirt back on.

"I'm in here," Joe said, unzipping the door of Maggie's tent and sticking his head out. "What's up?"

"Ronnie wants you. Some of the horses got spooked and ran away in the storm," Danny said.

"Thanks. I'll get right on it," Joe said.

"Come in, Danny." Maggie finger-combed her hair back into place.

"No, thanks."

His voice was accusatory, sarcastic. He knew exactly what had been going on.

"Danny, listen to me," Maggie pleaded, but she didn't know what to say. It didn't matter, Danny was gone.

"I have to go, Maggie." Joe turned toward her. "I'm sorry."

He was sorry? Sorry for what? For the best foreplay she'd ever had, or because they'd been caught?

Probably both.

She nodded. "Good night, Joe."

As he dashed into the rain, Maggie collapsed on her cot. What a mess. What a freaking mess.

Chapter Ten

Joe figured that he should just resign and let Ronnie or Quint take over Cowboy Quest. Or maybe one of his pals, Jake Dixon or Clint Scully, would have time.

He'd overstepped his bounds, and his actions were inexcusable.

He ran to where the rest of the horses were tied, and gave a loud whistle. He doubted if they could hear him over the storm, but he tried it anyway.

He noticed that the rest of the cowboys and some kids were also looking for the horses. He didn't want anyone to get lost, but he knew that his staff wouldn't let the kids out of their sight.

He whistled as loudly as he could, and Blue Bayou came back. Then Elmer. They were both spooked, and he turned them both over to their riders to pet them and calm them down. Lady was still missing, and from what he could tell, so was Checkmate.

Walking out farther into the woods, he gave another whistle, then another. Checkmate came, followed by Lady.

Ronnie ran toward him. "All are present now, boss."

"What the hell happened?"

"I don't know how they got loose. I know I tied them tight and secure."

"Do you think that the kids..." Joe couldn't finish. He would hate to think that the kids were responsible. If so, he hadn't done a good job so far of teaching them the Cowboy Code.

Ronnie adjusted his hat. "I don't know. Maybe. Maybe not."

"I'll take first watch," Joe said. "You get all the kids back into their tents."

Joe walked back to his tent for a quick change into better boots. It was a real possibility that some of the kids might have freed the horses.

That would mean that he was *really* failing. He was letting the kids down, letting the program down.

He shook his head, feeling like he was hanging on by the tail of his rope. With his mind focused on

Maggie so much, had he missed some of the signs that would indicate that the kids were unhappy or were planning to do something so potentially harmful to the animals?

And then Danny had found him in Maggie's tent. How could he be so stupid?

As the storm finally began to pass, Joe realized that the first problem he'd have to deal with was Danny Turner. But he also needed to speak with Maggie first. The two of them could present a united front and convince the boy that nothing was going on between them.

But that would be a lie.

He couldn't tell Danny that he'd lost himself in a crazy haze of lust. But his desire for Maggie was only partially what drew him to her. The truth is that he liked Maggie—a lot.

But he had his professional ethics to think about. Although her purpose in the program was a bit unusual, she was still in the program. He kept telling this to himself over and over, but clearly it wasn't sinking in.

Besides, she'd be hightailing it back to New York City just as soon as Cowboy Quest was over. There'd be no chance of getting to know her better…or even taking their relationship to the next level.

There *wasn't* another level. Maggie was off limits and would soon be headed out of Wyoming.

But that cliff was sure calling him over….

* * *

Maggie paced the length of her tent, worried about Danny and frustrated about Joe.

If she closed her eyes, she could feel Joe's lips on hers, feel the sensual slide of his tongue. How she'd wanted him. She still did.

But she'd never forget the expression on Danny's face—disbelief mixed with dread and anger. Before, she'd told him that nothing was going on between her and Joe—now she couldn't say that anymore.

Something *was* going on between them, but what?

Maybe the passion that they'd shared was just a spur-of-the-moment thing. The rain, the thunder and lightning and the small confines of her tent all made the perfect setting. Feeling Joe's strong arms around her, knowing that he wanted her...she hadn't been able to stop herself.

It was just a moment, she told herself. No big deal.

But it was a big deal where Danny was concerned.

She noticed the glare of a flashlight outside. Was it Danny returning?

"Maggie?"

Joe's voice penetrated her confusion.

She wanted to let him in, to finish what they'd started, but her common sense told her that it wasn't a good idea.

"Joe?" she asked. "Do you—?"

Water sluiced off the hand he held up, from his cowboy hat, down his slicker when she unzipped the tent flap. A flash of lightning outlined his strong body, reminding her of how it felt pressed against hers.

"I'm not going to come in. I just want to apologize."

Her heart did a dive. She didn't want him to express regret at what happened between them. *She* didn't regret what they'd done, only that their being together had upset Danny.

"There's nothing to apologize for."

"But you're in my program, and I shouldn't have—"

She wanted him to stop talking. "Go, get out of the rain. You're drenched."

"I'm on watch. You never know what mischief the kids can get into. Hopefully, they're tired enough to just sleep."

She nodded. "Well, good night."

"Good night." He turned to leave, then turned back on the next clap of thunder. "I think we have to talk to Dan the first thing in the morning."

"I know, and I'm dreading it."

It rained all night and a fine drizzle put a damper on the morning. Everything was muddy and wet. Maggie heard from Ronnie that a fight had broken out between two of the boys—Matt and Alex—that resulted in them rolling in the mud way too close to the horses' hooves.

"In my day, we'd put boxing gloves on both of them and let them duke it out," said Quint. "But apparently the state of Wyoming frowns upon that kind of thing these days."

"I'm going to let a jury of your peers figure out what to do with you two," Joe said. "The staff and I are going to butt out." He turned to the remaining participants. "So, I'd like the eleven of you to huddle quickly and decide on an appropriate punishment."

Maggie stood in the circle with the rest of the participants. In direct contrast from Matt and Alex wanting each other's blood a little earlier, the others were subdued and serious.

After a while, they settled on a punishment. Matt and Alex would have to work together putting up everyone's tents and taking them down for the next four days.

Maggie thought it was fair. And when she, as the elected jury foreman, told Joe their decision, he was more than pleased.

"I like it a lot, Maggie," he said. "It works on many levels."

"What worked was your idea of self-governing," she said, pushing back a wet lock of hair.

"Well, we'd better get going. Maybe we can

escape this rain." He looked up at the sky with its swirling wisps of black and gray clouds. "But it doesn't look good."

"We'll do the best we can."

He beamed and she thought her heart was going to melt.

But her mood dissipated when she remembered their kisses in her tent last night. It could never happen again.

She approached Danny. "Can we talk for a minute?"

"'Bout what?"

"About Joe and I and last night."

He shrugged. "You and the boss man can do what you want."

"Danny, it's not what you think—"

"I'm not stupid, Aunt Maggie. It's exactly what I think," he said. "And everybody here knows what's up. I hear about it all the time."

"They're still teasing you?"

"Yeah," he snapped.

Maggie laid a hand on his shoulder, and for once he didn't pull away. "I'm sorry. Do you want me to talk to Joe? He could get them to stop."

He looked at her in horror. "No! Don't do that. Don't do anything!"

"Whatever you want, but if it happens again, tell me and I'll handle it."

He shifted from one foot to another, and didn't answer. She knew he'd never snitch, as he'd call it.

"I apologize, Danny. It won't happen again. I don't want you to be teased, and I don't want to hurt you."

"I have to take care of my horse," he said, as if he hadn't heard her.

She dropped her hand from his shoulder. "I'll see you on the trail."

"Yeah." He turned to leave.

"Danny…" He turned toward her. "Just remember that I'm never going to leave you, and I'm never going to pick a man over you. I love you. Please believe me."

"Okay. See ya."

It seemed that his shoulders lifted a bit, and a worry line disappeared from his forehead.

Maggie made a promise to herself that she would always put Danny first. That's what he deserved, and that's where he belonged.

And that's what she owed her sister.

And if her being with Joe bothered Danny, she'd have to end their relationship.

The rain had stopped, and after breakfast Joe instructed the cowboys to move everyone out so they could get to their next camp-out point.

He'd arranged for Danny and Maggie to ride drag

with him, and motioned for them to hold back to let the rest of the train proceed.

"How's it going, Dan?" Joe asked.

"Okay."

"Making friends?"

"Some."

It was painful to talk to kids like Danny when they were tight-lipped and unresponsive. The boy had talked up a storm the day before, when they were leading the way.

"Dan, if you have something that's bothering you, I wish you'd tell me," Joe pushed.

Silence.

Maggie made a disgruntled noise. "You didn't like the fact that Joe was in my tent. Right?"

Silence.

"It's bothering you," Joe pushed. "Spill."

"How would you like it if everyone talked about you?" Danny snapped. "Called you Joe's pet and Joe's stepson? You wouldn't like it either."

"I know it's tough to have people call you names," Joe said. "But what's in it for them? Usually, they just want to press your buttons and watch you unravel."

Silence.

"Do you think I'm right, or not?" Joe asked. "I'd like to hear what you think."

"I don't know." He shrugged. "Maybe you're

right. Besides, what names would they ever call you? You're big. You can beat them up."

"I wasn't always this big. I was your age once, you know. And I was small for my age, like you."

"You were?"

"Yeah."

Maggie cleared her throat. "Danny, you know I'd never abandon you, don't you? Even if I date someone or go out with someone, I'll never leave you."

"Not even if you get married?"

"Not even then." Maggie smiled. "You're stuck with me, Danny. You might as well get used to it."

"Ignore the others," Joe said. "If you don't react, eventually they'll figure out that they're not getting to you, and they'll stop."

"You don't have to live with them. You don't have to be in this program," Danny said, quietly.

"What do you think you can do to not let them bug you?"

"I don't know. If I knew I'd do it."

"Let me ask you something first. Are you enjoying Cowboy Quest so far?" Joe asked. "Or do you still think it's lame?"

He shrugged his shoulders.

"C'mon, Danny. No one else is around. No one will think you're not cool. Talk to me and your aunt."

Danny leaned over to pet his horse. "I—I do like

Thunderbolt. And I like riding. And some of the guys are cool."

"But some aren't, and that's okay," Joe said. "And Cowboy Quest isn't perfect, huh? I understand that. But you like it."

He nodded.

"So why don't you accept the positive, ignore the negative and have a great time with your horse and with riding?" Joe could almost see the wheels turning in Danny's mind, so he continued. "And the rest is no one's business. Right?"

Danny met Joe's eyes for the first time. "Right."

"Cool. Anything else you'd like to get off your chest?"

"Nope."

"If there was, you could always write in your journal. Nothing like getting things off your mind by writing them down. Journal writing helps you sort things out by yourself if that's what you'd rather do. That's why journaling is part of Cowboy Quest."

"Yeah."

"Okay, Dan. Go hang out with your pals. And if you need to talk, I'm here."

"I'm here, too, Danny," Maggie said.

"Okay."

As Danny walked his horse forward to join his friends, Joe wondered if the boy really heard what he had to say, and if he could deflect—or ignore—the comments from his peers.

Joe figured that he could start a general discussion about peer pressure around the campfire. Maybe it would help Danny and some of the other boys.

He hated to single anyone out, but he knew he'd have to have another conversation with Brandon Avery. He couldn't prove anything yet, but he suspected that Brandon let the horses loose or was behind it somehow. Dan and Rick were probably involved, too.

"What do you think, Maggie?" he asked. "Did we reach him?"

"I'm almost positive that you did." She paused. "And you know, a few days ago I'd never have admitted even that. I didn't have much faith in you or your wranglers."

"And now?" Joe asked.

"Danny's at least listening to you."

"Have faith. It'll work out. Danny's a good kid. He has a lot of potential."

Maggie held up a hand, fingers crossed. "I hope you're right, Joe. I really do. I want to believe that more than anything."

Joe felt confident that the Danny issue would right itself, but what about Maggie and him?

He wanted her again. But how could they be together? He didn't want to sneak around. If they were caught, that would put her in another awkward situation with Danny and the rest of the boys.

But he couldn't think of any other alternative than for them to meet secretly—and hope that no one would find out.

Chapter Eleven

They started to see stray cattle later the next day.
The cowboys showed the boys how to slap their ropes
gently against their thighs to get the cows moving
together so they could take them to their summer
grazing grounds. Most of the cattle were branded
with SRR, for Joe's Silver River Ranch, though there
were many yearlings without a brand.

And just when she'd thought everything would
dry out, it started raining again.

She felt sorry for all the horses. They were slog-
ging through the muddy mess, yet it didn't seem to
bother them, or so she thought. Maybe they hated
it as much as she did.

Over the slopping of the mud and the splattering of the rain, Maggie thought she heard a noise, almost like the loud crying of a baby.

"Whoa, Lady. Whoa." The horse stopped, and she strained to listen. There it was again. Looking around, it didn't seem that anyone else had heard the pitiful cry.

"Joe!" she yelled, because he was the closest cowboy to her, but he didn't hear her. "Joe!" she yelled again. But the wagon train went on without her. She didn't dare go off on her own, especially in this weather.

She got a landmark fixed in her mind—a tall pine tree with a bent tip with a reddish-looking bush at its base. Then she coaxed Lady into a trot and hurried after Joe.

When she finally got to him, she was out of breath. "I heard this noise, Joe. Like a baby. Over there, Joe. Over there, in the trees." She pointed to an area to the left of them.

Several cowboys and kids joined them in the search. Eventually, they found the source of the bawling: a calf stuck in the mud. It looked exhausted from the struggle.

"Okay, Annie Oakley, it's time for you to do your roping." He turned toward her nephew. "Dan, how about if you lend a hand, too?"

"I'd like you both to see if you can rope the calf. Do you think you can do it sitting on your horse?"

Maggie nodded. Danny shrugged.

Maggie got her rope ready, made several circles and let it fly. It missed. There was a collective "Aww" from the spectators.

"Danny, you give it a shot," Joe said. "Maggie, try it again."

Maggie pulled in her rope. "Come on, Danny."

Danny's rope hit its target. When she tried again, hers did, too. Everyone cheered.

"Now, both of you, ride close together so you can pull the little guy out," Joe continued. "Go real slow. Let him get his footing. Slow."

Maggie smiled at Danny. He gave a nervous smile back. She could tell he was concentrating and didn't want to fail.

"You can do it," Joe said.

They walked their horses as slowly as possible, and a few moments later, the calf was able to walk out of the mud.

There were cheers all around and several high fives. Danny looked like he was sitting on top of the world. He needed this, Maggie thought.

She met Joe's gaze, and he winked at her.

Maggie gave her nephew a high five, and he returned it.

"Nice work, partner," she said.

"Nice work," he echoed, now grinning.

Joe took Maggie's rope off the calf, but kept Danny's on.

"Dan, slowly lead your new friend to the rest of the cattle. Maybe he'll find his mother."

Danny nodded and did as instructed. When he got to the herd that they'd gathered, he got off Thunderbolt, took the rope off the calf and gave it a quick pat. It scrambled off to join the others.

Danny looked back at her and smiled.

Maggie's heart swelled in her chest. Now she understood one of the components of Cowboy Quest—teamwork. That was the obvious message. The not-so-obvious one was that this little task had given her and Danny the chance to work together and do something they wouldn't normally do. The two of them together could accomplish anything if they tried.

Now what she needed to do was to apply this lesson to their life back home, in New York.

Home. It seemed so far away, yet she knew they'd be heading back all too soon, and she had to make some serious decisions about what to do. The stage had always been her ultimate goal, but lately it wasn't making her happy—not with Danny on her mind, knowing he needed her, knowing he needed a real parent. Yet she had to support them, and New York wasn't cheap.

She wondered again if she could make a living teaching dance and voice. Maybe, but she honestly wasn't sure.

This beautiful country did make her think. So

did the butt-numbing days on Lady. What else was there to do but move the cattle and think? Now if she could only make some decisions as to their future as a family…and whether or not she could continue performing. Then all would be well.

Wouldn't it?

They rounded up a good number of cattle throughout the afternoon. Joe thought that it would be a nice treat for everyone to stop early and take a dip—albeit a cold one—in a shallow branch of the Silver River. At least the water would be warmer in the spot that he'd picked.

He just didn't know what to do about Maggie.

"That's okay," she said, when he explained that the cowboys and their charges would be in a state of undress. "As long as I get my turn some time."

That would probably be at night.

Maggie stayed at the chuck wagon preparing the evening meal so even Cookie could go swimming.

Joe made it a point to try and talk to Brandon. Unfortunately, Brandon did everything in his power to avoid him. According to his records, Brandon's father was the chief of police in a small town in Montana, and Brandon was a constant embarrassment to his father. Brandon resented all authority, and acted out at every opportunity.

Nevertheless, Joe pressed on with the boy, almost resorting to hog-tying him to get him to stay put and listen. Finally, Brandon excused himself and went to be with his friends, including Daniel Turner.

And Joe couldn't help but think that they'd all have to get up pretty early in the morning to fool him. He knew all the tricks. He'd done them all and more.

Ronnie found a football and everyone had a great time diving and splashing through the water for the throws.

"You and your Aunt Maggie did a great job this morning," Joe said to Dan when the boy leaped for a clean catch. "That was fine roping and nice teamwork."

The boy's eyes scanned the crowd, probably noting who was watching him talk to the enemy.

"Thanks. It was…cool," Danny said. "Wait till I tell my homies."

"I thought you might decide not to run with your former pals when you get home. You know, the ones who got you into trouble in the first place. If you get probation, you won't be allowed to hang around with them. It'll be one of your probation rules."

Danny raised his arms and moved his hands in circles. "Are you telling me that I might get probation even after all of this?"

"Yeah, Dan, that's what I'm telling you. It all depends on what Judge Cunningham thinks. He might decide that you need the extra supervision that a probation officer can provide. You'd get an extra set of rules, and if you violate any of them, you could still be placed. You'd lose your aunt—and she'd be devastated."

Danny swore under his breath. "I'm screwed if I do good or not."

"That's not what I said. I said 'might' and 'maybe.' And remember that I have to prepare a report. Judge Cunningham will be looking at that. Can't you just be yourself? Can you be the person you were before you started stepping out and getting into trouble?"

He couldn't meet Joe's gaze. "I don't know if I can."

"Your aunt loves you very much, Dan. She really does. She'd do anything for you. Maybe some day you'll realize that, and give her a break."

Danny didn't say anything, but stood still and listened in spite of the fact that Quint threw the football an arm's reach away. The boy ignored it, but Joe scooped it out of the water.

"Think about what I said. Okay?" Joe asked, then pulled his arm back. "Now, go long, Dan."

He shot the football, and Danny leaped out of the water and caught it.

"Nice one!"

The dinner bell rang, and Joe motioned for them to dry off and get dressed. Everyone hated for the fun to end, but all the activity had made them pretty hungry.

When they got back to camp, the two boys who were on punishment for fighting were reminded that they had to put up the rest of the tents.

"I'll help you," said Mickey.

"Me, too," chorused Troy and Nick.

Fairly soon, all the other boys volunteered to help—with the exception of Brandon and Rick. Joe was happy that the boys were learning to work together, and made a mental note to give Brandon and Rick more cleanup duties.

Maggie had made chili and a salad, both of which went down well with the group. She beamed at the praise and Cookie even tried to pry the recipe out of her, but, laughing, she wouldn't budge.

Joe liked the fact that Maggie was getting the opportunity to cook. He remembered that she'd told him how much she enjoyed cooking, but never had a chance to do it.

And he loved to see her laugh. The worry lines disappeared from between her brows, and her whole face glowed. She was laughing more often, too.

After dinner, he assigned more duties. Cleanup and dishes to Brandon and Rick. Sleeping bag distribution to Matt and Alex. Cot distribution to two others. Then everyone would take care of their horses.

The whole camp would be busy, so Maggie could take a dip in the river.

He was afraid that she'd be too cold. "Are you sure that you want to do this?"

"Of course! I can't let you guys have all the fun."

"Okay then. I'll walk you there," he told her, leading the way through the trees.

When they reached the river, she sat down on a fallen tree, took off her boots and socks and waded gingerly into the water. "It's just as cold as I thought it'd be."

"Remember, this is Wyoming. I think that the snow just melted up here," he chuckled.

"Turn your back, please."

"Of course." The sun was setting, and he wanted to be closer to her. He sat on the fallen tree with his back toward the water, heard the rustle of clothes as she undressed and tried not to picture her naked.

He heard her gasp, and assumed that she'd gone deeper into the water.

"Yikes, it's cold," she said. "But it's really beautiful. Here I am, at sunset, wading into a spring-fed river with horses grazing in the distance… Life doesn't get any better than this."

"Oh?" He snickered. "What about the Met, Times Square, the lights of Broadway, Rockefeller Center?"

"Smog, concrete, noise, traffic, wall-to-wall people," she added.

He was surprised that she countered him.

"The New York Public Library, the museums, the restaurants, the—" He paused. "Hey, wait. Why am I praising New York City to you? I've been there all of…wait for it…*twice*."

"Really? What brought you to New York, Joe?"

"Madison Square Garden. I contracted with the Professional Bull Riders to supply some bulls for their event in January. That was a treat, driving my eighteen-wheeler full of my best bulls to the Garden and unloading right in front of the place."

"I didn't know they have a bull riding event at MSG."

He nodded. "Full house. You New Yorkers must love your bull riding."

"Next time you come to New York, I'll have to take you out on the town," she said.

"Next time I'll let you."

He heard more splashing, then footsteps and clothes rustling behind him once again—she must have gotten out of the water.

"You can look now."

She had changed into a pair of jeans and a hooded sweatshirt. Her feet were back into the boots, but her teeth had started to chatter from the cold. She shivered.

"It's too late in the evening for this," Joe said. "I should have known. You're freezing." He pulled her to him in an attempt to warm her with his body heat.

His hands traveled up and down her back, trying to rub some more warmth into her.

She looked up at him with her big emerald eyes and a smile that made her eyes twinkle, and that was his undoing. He gave her some time to tell him to stop, but she didn't.

His lips touched hers gingerly, and then harder. When he heard her softly say his name, he pulled her even tighter to him.

All the while, he was moving his hands over her body—to help warm her, he told himself. He shouldn't have let her swim this late in the freezing water, in the coolness of the setting sun.

Maggie's hands moved over his arms, his chest and his back. When her palms settled on the sides of his face, he thought he'd melt. She stared at him, smiling, happy.

It was Maggie who pulled him to her this time, her soft lips that touched his, gently, tentatively.

Exquisite torture, that's what this was, Joe thought, letting Maggie explore to her heart's content. It was all he could do to stop himself from finding a soft spot along the riverbank and making love to her.

But all too soon, he remembered all the reasons he couldn't.

He moved Maggie away from him, and dropped his arms. "Sorry. I shouldn't have done that. Forgive me."

"T-there's nothing to forgive," she said, her eyes opening in alarm.

"Yes, there is. I've overstepped my bounds—again." He ran a hand through his hair. "We should go—its getting dark."

He told himself that it was just kissing. But he knew that he wanted more from her—a lot more. He wanted her heart, body and soul.

But that didn't make any sense. He had experience with women who wanted more than he could offer, wanted more than hard work and long hours on a ranch.

He had absolutely nothing to offer a woman like Maggie.

But why was he even thinking about a long-term relationship? Why couldn't he enjoy her company now and forget about tomorrow?

Deep in his soul, he knew the answer to that. He wasn't a one-night stand kind of guy. When he gave his heart, he gave it forever.

But he couldn't give his heart to Maggie.

They didn't have forever. They only had what was left of Cowboy Quest, and her future with Danny was in *his* hands.

Chapter Twelve

Maggie shivered in the cold evening air. She desperately needed to wrap herself in several flannel shirts, sweats, maybe even a sleeping bag to make up for the loss of Joe's heat.

Yet again, he'd had an attack of guilt over a kiss. And she felt guilty about possibly hurting Danny.

She retrieved her old clothes from the fallen tree, and they walked back to the camp in silence. Maggie's face flamed when she remembered how she'd reacted to his kisses. She'd been lost in the moment, adrift on a sea of desire. She'd felt so right in Joe's arms.

She understood his point about him being in

charge of the program and that she was a participant, but who cared? To her dismay, she hadn't cared—not when his warm lips and hot mouth moved over hers. Not when she was gathered into his comforting embrace.

And she liked him—a lot. The big bear of a man was gentle, was good with kids and animals—what more could a woman want?

"Is there anything else you need, Maggie?" he asked.

"No. I'm fine. Thanks."

"No problem." He nodded and turned to leave.

"Uh, Joe?" He turned back. "Don't worry about the other thing, okay? It didn't mean anything." As soon as the latter slipped out of her mouth, she could have bit her tongue. "I mean—"

"I know what you mean." He walked toward his tent and shot over his shoulder, "I agree. It didn't mean anything."

His voice was steady, low, his shoulders set and rigid.

She didn't have a chance to explain that she'd never meant to hurt him—not for anything in the world.

They gathered up more stray cattle for the next two days. Joe kept his distance from Maggie, and when their paths did cross, he was overly polite. A businesslike atmosphere had replaced their easy camaraderie, and she felt alone and depressed. She wanted things back the way they were before.

Maggie had just finished riding night watch with Ronnie, Danny and Brandon. The four of them got along perfectly. For whatever reason, Danny seemed to be in good spirits without being sullen and distant, as did Brandon, and she wondered what that was about.

After an evening of singing show tunes (Maggie), country songs (Ronnie) and rap music (Danny and Brandon) to the cattle to calm them, they'd hit the sack when another team had taken over the watch.

On one occasion, in the distance, Maggie heard Brandon singing an old, romantic Elvis song. The kid was a fabulous singer!

When they arrived back at camp, she cornered him by the chuck wagon. "Brandon, I heard you singing, and you were wonderful. You have a very special gift."

"Thanks," he mumbled.

"Have you ever thought of singing professionally?" Maggie asked.

"Like at weddings?" he asked.

"Like on the stage."

"Me? Nah."

"Yes, you." Maggie insisted. Brandon didn't have any confidence in himself. "Do you play any instruments?"

"Guitar."

"Are you any good?"

"Sorta. Yeah," he replied.

"I'd love to hear you play and sing someday."

He shrugged. "Okay."

If it weren't so dark out, she'd swear that the toughest delinquent of the group was blushing.

After taking care of their horses, they all headed for the campfire where Quint was telling a ghost story. The plot sounded suspiciously like *The Phantom of the Opera*.

She took the only seat available, next to Joe.

"Would you like a cup of coffee?" he asked, holding up a blue speckled coffeepot that he'd just taken from the fire. "It's black, hot and horrible."

She shuddered. "Rust remover," Quint had called the deadly brew.

"Thanks, I'd love some," she said, figuring she'd never get to sleep tonight due to the overload of caffeine, but she just wanted to warm up. It was a chilly, damp night. She sank deeper into Joe's flannel shirt, which she had hardly taken off since he'd given it to her at her first riding lesson.

As she took the mug of coffee from Joe, her hands brushed his and he looked up into her eyes. It seemed like he was about to say something, but then his eyes shifted to all the people nearby and settled on the campfire.

She wanted him to tell her that he could feel the pull of desire between them, stirred by just a touch, but he didn't. Maybe something else was on his mind.

She took a sip of coffee and looked at Danny. He was in a huddle with Brandon, Jeff and two more kids. All three of them were hanging on Brandon's every word. Brandon looked over his shoulder at the string of horses, and Maggie wondered yet again if he'd had anything to do with the horses getting loose the first night. She could only hope her nephew wasn't involved.

She looked at Joe over the rim of her coffee cup. He seemed to be covertly watching the little clique, too. The other boys in the program were talking amongst themselves.

"Something's going on," she mumbled. "And I don't like the looks of it."

She felt a hand on her arm. Joe whispered, "I told you before, I'll take care of things. I'm aware that something's up. And I'm not the only one."

"What do you think it's about?"

"I think it's a jail break." He shook his head and tossed the remnants of his coffee onto the fire with a flick of his wrist. "And I think it's going to happen tonight."

"Where would they go? They don't know the area." A sick feeling crept into Maggie's stomach. "What are you going to do?"

"Nothing. I'm going to let it play out. Those who

are involved are going to have to pay the price," he said.

"But I'm afraid one of them will be Danny." Her stomach was roiling now.

"I'm afraid you're right."

A million scenarios were going through Maggie's head. She wanted to warn Danny by letting him know that everyone was aware that they were going to run away.

"Don't do it, Maggie," Joe said, as if he could read her mind. "Let him suffer the consequences of his behavior. Let him learn from his own mistakes."

"But I can't do that." She was going to be sick. "Aren't you supposed to help instead of making things worse?"

"Trust me. Do you think you can do that?"

"I don't want him hurt out there, riding in the dark. He's tired. We just got off watch, and—" She looked into Joe's onyx eyes, the hard planes of his face. There was a steely resolve about him, yet his gaze reflected tenderness and concern for her fears.

"I hope you know what you're doing," she finally conceded.

"I do." He sat back in his chair, and yelled over the talking. "Hey, how about a singalong, everyone? Maggie, will you start us off?"

It was lights-out, and everyone had adjourned to their respective tents. Maggie reluctantly went to hers, but Joe had a feeling that she wouldn't be sleeping.

She knew as well as he did that if the boys were up to something, it looked like it was going to happen tonight. He passed the word among his staff to let things unfold.

He felt the worst for Maggie. These kids weren't bad kids—they were just following Brandon who seemed determined to hold on to his bad streak. Joe didn't want Brandon to fail his program, but even he had to admit that he'd tried his best to get close to the kid, to no avail.

Brandon just wasn't ready yet. Even the lure of horses, campfires and camping didn't cut it for Brandon. He wouldn't be happy unless he was the leader of the pack.

Like tonight.

Well, tonight Joe was going to teach Jeff, Rick and Danny how *not* to be followers. Then, depending on how everything played out, it'd be Brandon Avery's turn to learn the responsibilities of a leader.

"Psst, Maggie. It's Joe."

She'd been tossing and turning for hours. Her pulse pounded in her ears as she went to unzip the flap. "What's wrong? It's Danny, isn't it?"

He nodded, and she thought her knees would give out. "Come with me, and don't make a sound."

He took her by the hand, and as they passed various tents, a couple of the cowboys stuck their heads out.

"Everything okay, boss?" Adriano asked, his gaze settling on their clasped hands.

"Just taking care of that little situation we discussed earlier," Joe said.

"If you need help, just give the signal."

"Will do."

Maggie wondered if the whole camp knew what was going on, everyone except her.

"Where are we going?" she finally asked, her mouth so dry that she could barely get out the question.

"To the remuda of horses." They ducked behind the chuck wagon and from their position, they were able to see four boys untying horses from the line.

Maggie could make out the tall, thin shape of a cowboy opposite them about fifty yards away—Ronnie. He was watching the action, too.

All kinds of things were going through her mind, including yelling to the boys and telling them to stop. But she stood there quietly, though it was the hardest thing she'd ever had to do.

Joe slipped a flashlight out of the pocket of his raincoat, as Maggie made a motion to walk toward the boys.

"Not yet," Joe said. "I'll let you know."

The wait was interminable. How much longer?

She wanted to scoop Danny up into her arms and hold him tight, never let him out of her sight again.

Then it dawned on her. She should have been doing that all along. But she'd been too overwhelmed by her own grief and confusion to focus on her nephew.

She could quit her job and find something else that she would enjoy just as much. But what would that be?

To even think of quitting the stage was remarkable. She used to think she'd never want to do anything else. But things had changed. It took standing in Wyoming in the wee hours of the morning, with the fear that Danny was going to go riding off in the dark with three other kids on horseback, to really make her think about what she could do differently.

They watched as the boys led the horses away from the camp. She had a feeling that bridles and saddles were stashed somewhere in the woods.

"Who's there besides Danny and Brandon?" she whispered.

"Jeff and Rick."

"I figured as much." She'd seen them huddled together enough times. Now she knew they'd been plotting and planning their escape.

"Why on earth would Danny want to run away?

From what I can tell, he's having the time of his life. He'd take Thunderbolt home if he could."

"I don't know if he really wants to run, or Jeff and Rick either. We'll see." He sighed. "I really thought that we'd made a difference."

He cared a lot about his program, about the kids. In spite of her worry about Danny, her heart was breaking for Joe. By the end of the night, his program could be very much in jeopardy.

Joe took her hand again. They crept along in the shadows until they saw the boys saddled up and astride their horses.

Maggie waited for Joe to say something. Instead, he held his index finger to his lips.

Were the boys crazy, trying to ride the horses in the dark? When was Joe going to call this off?

She felt his hand on the small of her back. He led her to the remuda. The boys were nowhere in sight now, but she could hear the horses moving through the woods.

The first voice she heard was Danny's.

"Brandon, this is a dumb idea. The horses can't see where they're going."

"Just shut up, Danny boy. I'm pretty sure that horses can see at night."

"Maybe we should have stolen a flashlight," someone said.

"I don't know why I'm doing this. It seemed like a good idea back at the bunkhouse, but now I'm not so sure," Danny said. "And I don't think that Thunderbolt can see in the dark. I don't think that any of the horses can. Let's go back, dude, before we're caught."

"Yeah, let's go back, Brandon," said Rick.

"I don't want to go back. I thought we weren't going to listen to that Cowboy Code crap anymore," Brandon said.

Silence.

"I don't think it's crap," Danny finally said. "I kinda like it. And I like Cowboy Quest."

"Me, too," said Jeff.

"It ain't bad," Rick said.

"Well, I'm going on without you weenies," Brandon said. "I'm outta here."

Brandon turned to leave, and the other three boys turned back toward camp.

Relief spread to all points of her body.

Now Maggie knew why Joe hadn't wanted her to interfere. If she'd jumped right in, Danny wouldn't have made his own decision.

And he made the right one.

"Thank you, Joe," she whispered. "I get it now."

"Hang on, you won't like what I'm going to do next." Leaping out of the trees he shined his flashlight on the three boys.

"I'd appreciate it if you got off those horses and led them back to the line," he said. "When the horses are tied up and groomed completely, and all the tack is cleaned and put away, then we'll talk."

"Yes, sir," came the response from the three boys.

Danny made eye contact with Maggie. "I'm sorry, Aunt Maggie."

His shoulders were slumped, and he looked like the loneliest little boy on the planet. He seemed so different from the arrogant, unemotional boy that he'd been for so long.

"We'll talk later," she said. "After you do what Joe said. You need to take care of your horse."

"Okay."

"Wait a moment, Dan." Joe handed Maggie the flashlight. "There's something wrong with Thunderbolt's back leg. He's limping."

Danny's eyes grew wide. "Will he be okay?" The boy's voice quivered, and he started petting the horse's neck as Joe inspected Thunderbolt's hoof. "I'm sorry, Joe. I'm really sorry," he whispered.

"He picked up a stone." Joe pulled his knife from its sheath and dug it out.

"You got lucky, Dan," Joe said. "Real lucky. If anything had happened to that horse…"

"I didn't think—"

"Go take care of Thunderbolt," Joe said sharply.

"Uh, Joe," Maggie said. "Aren't you forgetting

Brandon Avery? He has one of the horses, and he's in the dark."

"I didn't forget him." Joe whistled—*short, long, short*. Then he repeated the same. A couple of minutes later Brandon and his horse emerged from the woods. Brandon wore a confused expression on his face.

"First thing in the morning, there will be a jury of your peers," Joe said. "They'll cast a vote as to whether you'll be continuing on with Cowboy Quest."

Chapter Thirteen

Joe walked Maggie back to her tent. Due to her silence and her sporadic sighs, he could tell that she was mentally and emotionally exhausted.

"Things will work out. I have faith in the process," he said. "And I'm sure that all nine of you will come up with a fair punishment."

"Nine of us?" She swallowed hard. "You can't be serious. You expect me to be impartial when it comes to Danny? You know what's at stake, Joe."

"Matter of fact, I *know* you'll be impartial, Maggie. You and the other participants will come up with a fair and equitable decision as to what I should do with the offenders."

"But—"

He shrugged. "That's how we do it in Cowboy Quest. Now get some sleep. You look exhausted."

Her eyes were mere slits and the worry lines that had faded on the cattle drive were back. He wanted to hold her, kiss her, convince her that things would work out, but he'd vowed before that he wouldn't do that again.

Damn, it was hard.

She reached for his hand and held it. It was all he could do to stand still and not pull her toward him.

"No matter what happens, I'd like to thank you— for everything. Even though he blew it, I know that Danny has begun to change by the way he stood up to Brandon," she said, her eyes pooling with tears.

He had to leave or he was going to kiss the worry from her brow, kiss every inch of her.

"That's good to hear," he muttered. "Good night, Maggie."

She dropped his hand, and he felt a sense of relief…and disappointment.

The morning dawned bright and sunny, which didn't match Maggie's mood.

She didn't have a chance to talk to Danny, as she was assigned to help Cookie with breakfast. Danny was assigned to feed and water the horses, so they didn't see each other.

This was fine with her. She had passed being worried about him and had gravitated toward anger instead.

After breakfast, Joe stood. "I'd like each of the four boys that were involved to say whatever they'd like to say. Then the remaining nine participants will deliberate as to their consequences. Now, who would like to go first?"

Maggie decided that she was going to take a back seat in deliberations. Even though she was included as a participant, she wasn't impartial. She didn't want Danny to be eliminated from the program.

Jeff spoke first, then Rick. Neither had too much to say, but Maggie felt that they spoke from the heart when they said that they wanted another chance, and it was their decision, not anyone else's, to run off. They both added that they'd do anything to stay.

Then it was Brandon's turn. "I think Cowboy Quest is a joke, and I want out. And if my dumb horse hadn't turned around and gone back to camp, I'd be in Montana by now. I'd rather do my time than be stuck in this program with a bunch of wimps."

So much for Brandon's statement.

Then it was Danny's turn. Maggie held her breath.

"I am sorry for putting my horse, Thunderbolt, in danger by taking him out at night. I'd like to apologize to my Aunt Maggie, for many things. And to Joe. I think Cowboy Quest is pretty cool, and I didn't realize how much I'd learned until last night."

Maggie let her breath out. Danny stood tall, looking older than his thirteen years. Maybe it was because he was acting like a man.

Danny shifted on his feet. "I admit that I wanted to run from Cowboy Quest. I thought it was lame. But that was in the beginning, and I should have called off our plan—or my share in it. I'm not blaming anyone else but myself. I went along instead of backing out. And when Thunderbolt started limping—" Danny's voice caught. "Well, it would have been my fault if something happened to him. Anyway, I'll take whatever punishment, but I don't want to leave Cowboy Quest. I believe in the Cowboy Code, and I'm going to try to live up to it. That's all I got to say, I guess."

Joe stood. "I'd like the nine of you to discuss what kind of consequences should be given out. The rest of us will respect your decision as long as it's fair…so be fair."

She made eye contact with Joe, and he gave her a half smile. Damn, she liked this guy, and she liked his program, too.

"If Brandon doesn't want to be in the program, I say let him go home. What a jerk," said Kyle.

Marty nodded. "The other three finally stood up to him. They came back."

Alex, one of the two kids who'd been caught

fighting and ended up putting up every tent, spoke up. "I think Brandon should be sent home, and the other three should be given more work."

"What's the crummiest job here?" Maggie asked.

"Cleaning up horse crap...uh...excuse me Maggie," said a boy named Sean, with "love" and "hate" scratched onto his knuckles with ink.

"No need to excuse yourself, Sean. I agree wholeheartedly." She smiled at him, and he smiled shyly back.

The boys talked amongst themselves. They were taking their job seriously.

"One at a time!" someone yelled.

"What do you think, Maggie?" Cody asked. She remembered liking him when they were on cattle watch. He recited some poetry that he'd written about cattle.

"I think that you all know that Danny is my nephew, and I don't want to say much. I don't want to influence the group."

"I liked what he said."

"Yeah. Rick and Jeff, too."

"But what do we do with them?"

"Let them muck stalls forever. Then we don't have to."

"Yeah!" There were high fives all around.

"And send Brandon home."

"Yeah." This time there we no high fives and no cheers.

That was the verdict they delivered. Joe's perfect record was now gone. One failure.

The other three boys were relieved and nodded vigorously when told that they would clean up after the horses for the rest of their stay.

And Maggie thought that Brandon didn't look as haughty as he had before.

"Are you okay with the verdict, Joe?" Maggie asked Joe when they were back on the trail.

"I think that the system worked again," he said. "Although I wouldn't want to muck for the rest of the program, it's a good punishment."

"Too bad about Brandon," Maggie said.

"I haven't given up on him. After he gets a dose of placement, maybe I can negotiate an early release and get him back to Cowboy Quest. Brandon has the potential to be a leader, if he'd only turn himself around."

"He ruined your perfect record."

He nodded. "As much as I hate to have my record ruined, it's only a statistic. I'm not going to win over every kid. Brandon is a young boy. And he reminds me a lot of myself when I was his age."

"And you're going to take him under your wing, aren't you? Just like Mr. Dixon did for you?"

Joe smiled. "Looks like Danny's doing well at the moment, and Brandon is faltering. So if you'll excuse me, Maggie, I'm going to have a heart-to-heart discussion with Brandon as we ride. Then I'm going to talk to Jeff and Rick. Maybe you'd like to do the same with Danny."

She smiled. "I would, Joe. Thanks."

Lightly tapping her rope on her thigh to keep the cattle moving, she rode her horse to where Danny was doing the same. She remembered a time when she'd been scared to ride.

She still couldn't believe how much she liked riding Lady and being out in the fresh air—well, it'd be fresher without the cattle. And it had taken something as serious as Danny's problems to bring her here.

She hadn't seen much of the world, and she decided that she'd like to see more of Wyoming and other parts west with Danny, if her schedule permitted. But when she got back, she'd have to see what her agent could find for her to do.

She sighed. As much as she'd dreaded coming here, she dreaded going back to the same old grind—rehearsal, memorizing lines, songs and musical numbers and practicing until she could do them in her sleep. Then there were all the unresolved issues with Danny—they still had a lot of work to do on their relationship.

Maggie felt a familiar ache between her shoulder blades. She just wanted more time away before she had to go back to the stage.

She had some savings socked away, and maybe she and Danny could take an extended trip. School would be out in a month, and his classes here were going better than she ever dreamed possible. Maybe they could tack on another two weeks.

Danny noticed her riding in his direction, and he gave her a weak smile. No doubt he was expecting a lecture from her.

Boy, was he going to be surprised.

She wasn't going to lecture. Danny had already figured out what he'd done wrong.

A light rain had started, and she hurriedly pulled her poncho from her saddlebag and slipped it on. She noticed the rest of the boys doing the same.

"Good morning, Danny!"

He looked at her warily. "Aunt Maggie...uh... hello."

"Sleep well?"

"Yeah...well, no."

"Oh? Why not?"

"I was thinking," he said.

"About...?"

"About how I shouldn't have tried to run away like that."

"Where were you going anyway?" she asked.

"Canada."

"Canada? That's a long way away on horseback," she said.

"We were going to hot-wire a car."

"But Danny, that would be another crime on your record! And what about Thunderbolt and the rest of the horses?"

"I didn't want to leave Thunderbolt alone." He looked at her, meeting her eyes for the first time. "I didn't want to leave any of the horses. I couldn't do that. And I didn't...*don't* want to be placed at an institution."

A feeling of relief washed over her, and she relaxed in the saddle. "It's good that you're thinking of the horses, and being placed. Now take it one step further and think of me. How do you think I'd feel if something happened to you?"

"I—I don't know."

"I'd be devastated, Danny. You mean the world to me. I couldn't stand it if you got hurt or..." She couldn't finish the sentence.

Tears started a slow trail down her cheeks, and she quickly brushed them away.

"Are you crying?" Danny asked.

She nodded.

"About me?"

"Yes, and it isn't the first time, Danny."

"I'm sorry, Aunt Maggie. I really am. And I don't want you to cry anymore."

She wished they were on land instead of on horseback, so she could hug him.

"I love you, Danny."

"I love you, too."

She tried not to cry, she really did, but she couldn't help herself. She'd waited to hear those three wonderful words since she took custody of Danny two years ago.

"These are happy tears," she assured him when he frowned. "Really."

Danny chuckled, then a shocked expression appeared on his face. "What's that noise?" He slanted his head to the left, as if straining to hear. "Something's wrong, Aunt Maggie."

Then she heard it, too. Thunder?

"Stampede!" Joe yelled. "Everyone, get out of the way. Follow Ronnie and Quint! Head for the trees! Now!"

Ronnie let out a whistle—short, long, short—and the horses turned to follow him and Quint. Eventually, all thirteen horses hurried up the hill. Maggie's heart pounded just as loudly as the running of the herd.

In the pouring rain, they all watched the action safely from their position.

The rest of the cowboys gave chase. Maggie held her breath, watching how Joe galloped alongside the cattle. He gripped the horse with his knees, leaning forward, swinging his rope and slapping it against a rock-hard thigh.

He was racing to the front of the herd, which consisted of approximately three hundred cattle and calves that they had picked up. More seemed to be joining in the fray, but that was probably her imagination.

The remaining cowboys also raced to the front of the herd.

"Wow!" said Danny. "I wish I could do that."

"Me, too," Maggie agreed, surprising herself. "I mean, I wish I could ride like that." Funny, less than a month ago even sitting on a horse was the furthest thing from her mind.

As she watched Joe, she saw no distinction between rider and horse—they moved together as one. His strong thighs gripped the sides of the horse as he leaned forward, trying to get in front of the cattle. His black hair, tied back in a ponytail, blew in the wind.

"Go, Joe!" yelled Ronnie.

Quint took his hat off and waved it over his head. "C'mon, boss!"

When Joe finally got to the head of the herd, he cut across.

"What is he doing, trying to kill himself?" Maggie shouted over the noise.

"He's turning the leaders around," Ronnie said.

"Turning the leaders around..." Maggie repeated. "That's interesting."

Suddenly Maggie had a brilliant idea as to how they might be able to turn Brandon around. And she couldn't wait to share it with Joe.

* * *

Joe blinked the rain from his eyes. He and the other cowboys had gotten the cattle turned, and now the herd was milling around, looking as docile and harmless as stuffed animals. But he knew they'd be jumpy all night and for a good portion of tomorrow.

He knew what had spooked the cattle enough to stampede all right—everyone shaking out their plastic rain ponchos at once. It must have sounded like gunfire to the poor beasts.

He saw Maggie and the kids on elevated ground with Ronnie, who gave him the thumbs-up sign. He said a silent prayer of thanksgiving that everyone was okay.

"Is everyone all right?" he asked.

There was no response to the contrary.

Maggie's hair was pin-straight, the ends wet with rain, and she looked beautiful. She gave him a big smile and said, "That was some riding, Joe."

He chuckled. "Thanks."

"Yeah, Joe. Way cool," said Danny.

Everyone else was in agreement. Clint and Ronnie each gave him a half smile, raised their eyebrows and excused themselves to work the cattle. Joe couldn't help but laugh at the mocking expressions on their faces. Any of the cowboys could have turned the herd.

But Joe relished Maggie's look the most, a

combination of admiration and awe. He could almost believe that he was a hero in her eyes, but she was probably just overwhelmed after experiencing her first stampede.

"What about you, Joe, are you okay?" she asked. "You were the one in harm's way."

"I'm doing great, Maggie." He was high on adrenaline. When he crashed, he was going to have a wicked headache. "How about you?"

"Oh, we're all fine. It was a little scary, but Ronnie and Quint got us all out of the way, just as you ordered."

"Good." All their training, for just such a problem, had worked.

Looking up at the sky, he noticed that the sun was peeking out of the clouds. It'd be a nice day tomorrow—finally.

"Let's pitch camp here. I'm going to double up on watch tonight. I'll give you your assignments after you take care of your horses. And tonight I want some nice, quiet singing to keep the cattle calm. They're going to be jumpy after the stampede. I don't care what you sing as long as it's quiet."

Maggie raised her hand. "Joe, can I speak to you for a moment?"

"Sure."

She got down off Lady and walked toward him, holding the horse's reins. She didn't speak, but seemed to be waiting for everyone to make their way toward the chuck wagon and the herd. Ronnie had already strung a rope between two trees for the remuda.

She spoke after the last rider was out of hearing distance. "I have a favor to ask you."

"Fire away."

"Would you assign me night watch with Brandon? And Danny, too."

"Should I ask why?"

She grinned. "Because I have a scathingly brilliant idea. I think I know how to turn Brandon Avery into a leader."

Chapter Fourteen

"Tell me about your plan, Maggie."

"You should hear Brandon sing, Joe. The kid has talent. He told me that he could play the guitar, so I'm going to ask Cookie if we can borrow his. I want to see what Brandon can do. I think that using his talent would help him. With something positive in his life, maybe he won't need to act out so much."

"That's good thinking, Maggie. I like it a lot, and I think it's great that you're taking such interest in him." Joe looked at her and tilted his head.

"But you haven't heard the best part. I think we should put on a talent show. Nothing big, just for us. Maybe one night around the campfire."

"And you're going to get Brandon to sing and play the guitar?"

"I am. I've taught kids in the past, and I've done a good job if I say so myself. Maybe I can help him polish his performance."

He nodded. "Go for it. I'm for anything that would give Brandon a positive experience. I thought it'd be Cowboy Quest, but he wants out, and you and the kids voted him out. I have to respect that."

"But there's no deadline on when he has to leave, right? So until then, you're not giving up on him, are you?"

"Not by a long shot."

They walked their horses toward the others. "How are you and Danny doing?" Joe asked.

"We had another nice conversation going before the stampede. He's opening up more and more."

"Excellent." She thought he was about to take her hand, but he seemed to change his mind. As much as she wanted him to, they were too close and everyone could see. And Joe had made it clear that they weren't going to be a couple, and that was fine with her. She had too many things on her mind.

Still, she couldn't help but feel as though she'd lost something special.

She looked over at Brandon, sitting by himself for dinner. She felt sorry for the boy. Brandon was acting like he didn't care, but that was a façade, the same defense mechanism that Danny always used.

She wanted to help Joe help the boy. And she felt that the talent show would give all the kids the confidence boost they needed.

As they walked, she could see Danny, Rick and Jeff working hard, cleaning up after the horses. Danny was laughing, and it didn't appear that his punishment was that much of a hardship at all. She smiled. Joe had promised hard work, and he'd lived up to his promise.

She felt his hand at the small of her back. "The talent show is an excellent idea, Maggie. Whatever you need, let me know."

The boys are getting restless, Maggie thought. Several days of riding were taking their toll. Joe must have sensed it, too, because he soon suggested a cowboy triathlon for the kids.

When he announced that the triathlon would consist of a horseshoe tournament, a roping match and a contest as to who could bridle and saddle his horse the fastest, the boys were thrilled. When he announced that there would be prizes, a cheer went up from the group.

"Maggie, unless you want to participate, would you mind assisting me in keeping score?" Joe asked.

Maggie waited for Danny's reaction to Joe's request, but he just smiled. She didn't know if he was simply happy to participate in sporting events for prizes, or if he was getting over the fact that Joe was singling her out.

"I'd be happy to keep score," she said. "Let me get some paper and a pen."

She knew that Cookie would have what she needed, so she headed for the chuck wagon.

When Maggie returned, she couldn't help but observe Joe. He was in his element, giving instructions, dividing the group into teams. She watched how his muscles moved under his blue-striped shirt, and the way his features changed from intense concentration to hearty laughter and twinkling eyes.

When the horseshoe tournament was under way, the boys cheered for everyone, not only their team. Maggie could see that it was Joe who slanted that result by cheering for each individual and the boys followed his lead.

After Team B won the tournament, Joe promised them all their own rope. Team A was visibly disappointed.

"Hang in there, Team A. We have two more events," he said.

He looked over at Maggie and winked. She winked back. She knew that Joe would see to it that everyone would receive a prize.

That fact warmed her all over. When he stood

close to her during the roping event, she could smell the aftershave that he used. It reminded her of their kiss, and butterflies settled in her stomach. Her glow faded when she remembered that the clock was ticking, and soon Cowboy Quest would be over.

Could she handle not seeing Joe again?

As luck would have it, Team A won the roping event, and they all would receive their own rope, too.

The bridling and saddling of the horses would be the tiebreaker. Joe timed each individual and told her the results. As she totaled up each column, she noticed that he managed to make the results come out even.

He announced that both teams would receive Western shirts as prizes, and there were cheers all around. But Joe had something up his sleeve.

"To break the tie, I'd like the individuals with the lowest scores from the saddle-and-bridle event to run through the triathlon again," he announced. "The two individuals would be... Maggie, who had the lowest scores?"

Her heart did a leap in her chest. Danny was one. Then she ran her finger down the other column. Brandon was the other.

When she told Joe this fact, he didn't seem surprised. He'd planned this.

She tried not to cheer too loudly for Danny, but

was thrilled when Danny won the horseshoe event. Brandon won in roping.

She doubted that Joe could pull off another believable tie, and she found herself holding her breath during the last event.

Since it took Danny two tries to swing the saddle up on Thunderbolt, Brandon won easily.

"Brandon, you are the all-around champion of the Cowboy Triathlon. You are the grand-prize winner of a gold buckle."

Everyone cheered. Brandon smiled and accepted pats on the back from all the boys. Then when the excitement died down, he turned to Joe.

"I can't accept the gold buckle, Mr. Watley," Brandon said, his eyes meeting Joe's. "I'm not part of the program anymore, and I shouldn't have competed."

Maggie's heart melted. This certainly was a change in the boy.

"I appreciate that you feel that way, but why don't we ask the other members of Cowboy Quest to render a decision? If it is decided to disqualify you, then Danny wins the gold buckle."

She looked at Danny. His eyes lit up, but he tried not to react. She could tell that he wanted that buckle.

Joe turned to her. "You need to participate in the vote, too, Maggie. You're part of Cowboy Quest. Dan, you'll sit it out, since this vote directly affects you, too."

"But—" Maggie began. How could she tell Joe that she wasn't comfortable participating in this verdict? But after an encouraging nod from him, she joined the group at the chuck wagon.

The discussion began all at once.

"Brandon won fair and square."

"But he's right. He shouldn't have competed."

"He's changed. He's not like before."

"I think he should keep the gold buckle."

"But what would Danny get?"

"Nothing, I guess."

"That ain't fair."

Maggie didn't say anything until someone asked her point-blank.

"This is a tough one," Maggie said, looking at the serious boys. "But Joe didn't disqualify Brandon from participating in the triathlon, so he competed fair and square."

"Yeah. Maggie's right."

"Let's take a vote!"

In the end, it was voted that Brandon keep his prize. The boy looked like he was about to cry or bolt, and Maggie didn't want him to do either.

"Thanks guys…and you, too, Maggie," he said humbly. "I never won anything before."

There were more cheers and clapping.

She smiled at Brandon and patted his shoulder. "Congratulations."

Maggie was proud of Danny for shaking

Brandon's hand and cheering as loudly as the others.

Joe waited until the excitement died down, then he held his hands up for quiet. "The second-place prize, which is a saddle, goes to Dan Turner."

Danny looked like Joe just handed him a million bucks. When the boys were busy cheering, he made eye contact with her. This time, she winked first.

His head tipped back, and he laughed. He moved next to her and their hands touched. She wanted to hold his hand, kiss him and never let him go. But she didn't dare do either.

Maggie looked up at him. "Join me for dinner, cowboy?"

"Do you think it's okay?"

She looked over at Danny, happier than she'd seen him in a long time. Thinking about their previous talk, Maggie believed that she'd gotten through to Danny, that he finally realized that she'd never shut him out of her life.

It was time to see if he could be okay with her being with Joe, but she had faith in Danny that he could handle it.

She smiled at Joe. "I think that it's perfectly okay."

Later, over a dinner of hamburgers and salad, Danny joined them. She didn't care if he liked it or not, but she gave him a hug then a kiss on the forehead.

"Aww..." He squirmed.

She noticed Joe watching her, grinning.

In spite of the temperature, heat rushed to her cheeks and her stomach tingled. She realized that whenever he looked at her or she thought about him, that same thing happened.

She was falling in love with Joe.

That should have made her happy, and it did—in a way. But how on earth could they ever make a long-distance relationship work? Besides, deep down, she knew she was a lot like the ex-fiancée who'd left him for a life in Los Angeles.

She knew he'd never move to New York. He was a cowboy through and through, and his life was here. Just like her life was in the city.

An overwhelming sadness settled in her heart.

How could she ever leave him?

All too soon it was time for the night watch. To her surprise, she was riding with Joe. True to his word, he'd assigned Brandon to ride in their group, along with Danny.

Overly tired, she didn't know how she'd stay awake, but the fact that she was going to talk to Brandon gave her renewed energy.

She found her opportunity when she heard Brandon singing to the cattle. It was a sad country ballad that she'd heard before, but couldn't place the artist.

She slowly rode over to him. "You are really, really good, Brandon. I mean that."

When he smiled, the harsh lines disappeared from his face, and he looked younger.

"Brandon, there's going to be a little talent show by the campfire at the end of the roundup. Would you be interested? I asked Cookie, and he agreed to lend you his guitar to practice on. What do you say?"

"I don't know…"

"If you'd like, I'll help you."

"You will?" His eyes were as big as one of Joe's belt buckles.

"Of course I will."

"Cool."

"So would you like to be in the talent show?" she pushed.

"It's lame, but yeah, I'll do it."

"Terrific." She lowered her voice. "Brandon, you'd like to stay in Cowboy Quest, wouldn't you?"

He didn't say a word, but just nodded. Then he rode away.

Feeling higher than the big moon in the sky, Maggie rode over to Danny to spend the rest of the night watch with her nephew.

Late that night, Maggie gathered up a towel and some clean clothes and quietly slipped out of her tent. She desperately wanted to dunk herself in the sparkling water of the Silver River. She was surprised at how long the river was—it went on for miles, cutting through Joe's property, ravines, hills and valleys. But right now, she was thinking of the spot that she'd seen earlier—a bend in the river that made a natural whirlpool.

When she got there, someone else was in her spot.

Joe.

He sat in the whirlpool, whistling. She was an intruder to his solitude, a voyeur—who couldn't move if her life depended on it.

"Looks like we had the same idea," he said, spotting her.

"I should leave." But her feet felt like they were hardening in cement. "I'm sorry to intrude."

"There's room enough for us both," he said. "It's a big river."

She couldn't join him, could she? She couldn't strip down and walk into the water and be that close to Joe. She'd want to touch him and feel his hard muscles under her fingertips, feel his taut skin under the palms of her hands.

She was just about to tell him that she couldn't when he held out his hand to her. "Come here, Maggie."

He stood, naked. Water dripped off his hair and into little rivulets that trailed down his strong body.

As if in a trance, she walked toward him, dispensing with her clothes piece by piece. She slipped off her bra, her panties, and waded into the water as if a camp full of kids and cowboys wasn't just over the rise behind them.

Please don't let anyone see us. Please just give me this one night with Joe.

He gathered her up into an embrace. She could feel his hardness, pressing against her, getting harder still. As her heart pounded, he kissed her neck, her forehead, then his mouth took hers in a hungry kiss like no other she'd ever experienced. She felt more alive than she'd felt in years, more alive than she ever felt on the stage.

She ran her hands over his hard chest, tangled her fingers in his ponytail, traced a tiny stream of water down his chest until it disappeared.

"I want you, Maggie. I've wanted you for a long time."

"I've wanted you, too, but—"

"No buts, not tonight."

He grabbed at the soap, floating in the water. He scrubbed every inch of her, rubbing, tracing, touching. They played, they splashed, they kissed and when she finally wrapped her legs around him, they were silent for a moment.

"If you're going to say no, Maggie, now's the time."

"I'm not."

He kissed one nipple, then the other, teasing them with his tongue. She couldn't stop saying his name.

And when he entered her, she bit her lip to stop from screaming. He felt so, so good.

She caught her breath, matched him stroke for stroke, until they moved in a rhythm of their own.

They fell over the cliff together, free-falling in time and space until they landed back in a small whirlpool somewhere in the middle of Wyoming.

No matter what, this was a place she'd never forget.

And she'd never forget Joe Watley.

Besides, what was the sense in playing "what if"? Her life was fine dining and high-rises; his was wide-open spaces and cowboy coffee. She was designer clothes and car services; he was flannel and horses. She had Danny; he had Cowboy Quest.

They didn't stand a chance.

Chapter Fifteen

Joe knew he had to remove the silly grin from his face before he walked back into camp.

The kids weren't stupid and neither was his staff.

He'd tried to stay away from her, he really had. But when he'd seen her, bathed in the moonlight, watching him...he'd wanted her.

It felt so right holding her in his arms, making love with her. He was happy with Maggie. Happier than he'd been in a long, lonely time.

He even thought that he loved her.

But happiness took a dive when a picture of Ellen Rogers flashed into his mind. He'd loved Ellen, too, and she'd left for the lure of the big city. And Maggie lived in the most vibrant city in the world, with a glamorous job to boot. She was a *star,* for Pete's sake.

He'd sworn he wouldn't risk his heart on a woman like this ever again.

Too late.

That wiped the silly grin off his face.

"Joe, we have a problem." Ronnie came running up to him. He nodded in Maggie's direction. If he noticed anything, he didn't let on.

Ronnie shook his head. "Danny's missing. So is Brandon."

Joe's stomach turned. This couldn't be good.

"Oh, no!" said Maggie, running to the camp with Ronnie and Joe.

"What happened?" Joe asked.

"Seems like they went to the latrine and they never came back," Ronnie said.

"Are all the horses here, Ronnie?"

"Yes. Wherever the boys are, they're on foot."

"What can I do, Joe?" Maggie asked, fear in her voice. "I can't believe he'd run away again." She took a deep breath to steady herself. "If I lose Danny…"

He took her by the arms. Her hair was still wet, and he didn't want her to catch a cold.

"Don't think that way," he said. "Get a coat on, and follow me. Hurry."

The cowboys had gathered by the campfire, carrying flashlights and ropes. He assigned three of them to stay with the remaining boys.

"Maggie, Ronnie and I will head for the ravine. The rest of you fan out in teams of two from here. If you find them, give a yell and use this." He handed out flare guns.

He took Maggie's hand and led her north, toward the ravine, through a dense forest of lodgepole pines and other evergreens and conifers. The thick carpet of needles kept them somewhat out of the mud.

"Are you okay, Maggie?" That was a stupid question.

"I'm doing okay, but I'm worried to death."

"Of course you are, but we'll find them." Joe took a deep breath. There were all kinds of animals in these woods: bears, mountain lions... He touched his gun. He'd hate for the boys to come across any of those.

"Help!"

The sound was faint, but he'd heard it. "Stop. Listen."

"Help!"

"It's coming from over there." Ronnie pointed.

"Danny?" yelled Maggie.

"Yes!"

"Keep yelling," Joe ordered.

By flashlight, they found Danny crouched, looking down a fifty-foot ravine. Brandon was standing at the bottom.

"Brandon, are you okay?" Joe shouted.

"I'm fine. I just can't get out of here. The bank is slippery and wet and I can't grab onto anything."

"I forgot my rope, Joe," Danny said. "You said that a cowboy should never be without his rope. I don't have it."

The boy was scared for his friend. Joe handed him his rope. "We'll get him out of there."

"Don't be mad at Brandon, Joe. It's my fault. I'm the one who went off the path. I thought I heard a calf, but it was a deer and—"

"We'll talk about it later," Joe said, putting his hand on Danny's shoulder to calm him. "What do you think we should do, Dan?"

"I think I should go down there and help Brandon. It's my fault that this happened."

He looked at Maggie, and she was ready to shake her head no, but changed her mind when she saw his expression.

"Okay, Dan. We're going to take our ropes and go hand over hand and walk backward down the bank. We aren't going to rappel down or do anything fancy. We're just going to take it slow. Okay?"

"Got it," Danny said.

Joe walked over to Maggie. "Remember, I'm a paramedic and so is Cookie. And I can get a chopper here in minutes. Don't worry." Cookie handed him a gear bag full of supplies he might need.

"Boss, there's a harness in there, and pulleys and

hitches," Cookie said, walking over to Joe. "And I brought a litter. Just in case."

Ronnie fired his flare gun. More help would be coming. If Brandon needed to be taken to a hospital for whatever reason, he'd phone Jake Dixon to chopper in, but he hoped that wouldn't be necessary.

As he and Danny tied ropes around their waists, the cowboys wrapped the other ends around a tree trunk several times.

"Remember, we're not going to rappel down, Dan. We are going to take this nice and slow. Backward. Hand over hand. Watch me first."

Joe anchored the gear bag around himself and demonstrated how he wanted Danny to walk backward down the rope line.

"Be careful, Danny."

"I will, Aunt Maggie."

"I know you will, but I had to say it anyway. It's my job."

Danny laughed nervously, and so did the others who were standing nearby. It cleared some of the tension.

"Ready?" Joe asked. He'd climb down first so if the boy got into trouble, he'd be there to help him.

Slowly, they climbed down the side of the ravine until they were next to Brandon.

"Nothing broken, Brandon?"

"Nope."

"By any chance, are those steel-toed boots?"

Joe asked, still checking the boy for broken bones, grateful that Jake Dixon had advised him to take EMT training if he was going to work with kids.

Brandon smiled. "Yeah."

"Smart."

Joe couldn't find anything wrong with him. "We're going to slip both of you guys into a harness. Then we'll secure a couple of pulleys and hitches, but mostly the guys upstairs will pull us up. Okay?"

"Okay. Thanks, Joe," Brandon said.

"I'm sorry, Brandon. I thought it was a calf," Danny said.

"For what? You didn't do anything. The mud just washed away, and I slid down. I'm glad you didn't leave me."

"I couldn't do that."

Joe cupped his hands over his mouth and yelled. "Pull him up. Nice and slow!"

Joe let out a long breath of relief. "Brandon, just grip the rope and walk up. The others on top will pull you up. Dan, you'll go next."

When they got to the top, Joe was astonished to see that those who were pulling the ropes were none other than the Cowboy Quest kids, with Maggie at the front of the line. His staff was cheering them on.

Warmth washed over him when he saw Brandon in the middle of his peers, receiving pats on the back. Brandon was shaking hands with everyone, graciously thanking them for their help.

After Brandon told them about Danny's part in the rescue, Danny was hoisted on their shoulders and there were more cheers.

"Atta boy, Dan!" yelled Quint.

When they finally let Danny down, Maggie hugged him tightly to her. "Don't ever go off like that on your own again. Do you hear me?"

He nodded and hugged her back, smiling.

Brandon walked over to Joe with his hand extended. "I'd like to thank you, Joe. And I'm sorry again for screwing up."

Joe took Brandon's hand and shook it, then pulled the boy toward him in a hug.

He knew that he'd have to have a conversation with the two boys about straying from camp, lost calf or not, but now was not the time.

He glanced at Maggie. Huddled in her coat, she seemed cold, and he wanted to take her in his arms and make her warm.

Later in her tent, he intended to make her that offer.

The next evening, Maggie watched as the boys brought wood for the campfire and stacked it in the fire ring. She checked her clipboard and was pleased to note that everyone had signed up to do something. Even the cowboys were going to sing, do magic tricks, tell stories.

They all needed some fun. Two more days of roping and branding calves, aching bones and night watch left everyone mentally and physically drained.

She'd taught Danny how to do the Texas Skip, and listened to Brandon's singing and guitar playing and made some suggestions. She was so impressed with his obvious talent that she'd asked him to perform two songs in the show. She could tell by his shy smile that he was flattered by her praise.

Maggie was anxious to return to the Silver River Ranch. She couldn't wait to sleep in a real bed and use a real bathroom, but she'd definitely miss the whirlpool that she'd shared with Joe.

Smiling, she thought of how they'd quietly made love again in her tent last night. His hard, taut body moved over hers, his kisses were warm and tender, sometimes hard and demanding, and he was attentive to her every need. They moved together like longtime lovers, yet when they made love it was new, fresh and romantic, and she'd never felt more alive.

From what she'd observed firsthand, Joe's Cowboy Quest program was an overwhelming success. He was an honorable man, an advocate for children, a skillful lover, a profitable rancher and stock contractor.

And she loved him.

But Joe had never expressed feelings for her. Maybe she was just a fling for him. Since their lives were so different, why should she expect anything more?

She couldn't think about this now or she'd go crazy. She had a show to put on.

The boys and the cowboys were grouped around the campfire. There were no more cliques that she could tell. Cowboys and kids were all mixed together, and she was sure that Joe noticed this, too. He didn't miss a thing.

She announced Brandon and his first song. His voice drifted around her, clear and true. It was a song about losing love then finding it again, set to an urban beat. Even though she'd heard it several times before, this time it spoke to her, reminding her of her situation with Joe.

Tears pooled in her eyes when Brandon got a standing ovation from everyone, led by Danny. Brandon looked like a deer in the headlights, frozen and stunned. It took him a while to recover to sing his other selection.

Not such a tough guy anymore, she thought. Brandon just needed positive reinforcement and some real friends, people who liked him for himself.

Danny performed the Texas Skip with only a couple of good-natured blunders that had everyone laughing at his reaction. He, too, got a great cheer and several of the boys made him promise to teach them.

Joe did some knot-tying, passing out rope for everyone to try. "Now we'll do the rolling hitch. It's used to fasten a rope to a post." He did the bowline knot, half hitches and the water knot. The cowboys assisted everyone and it was a lot of fun.

Buckets of popcorn, gallons of water and hundreds of s'mores later, Joe finally called for lights-out. "Tomorrow we'll head back to the ranch. It'll be two days on the trail, weather permitting, and it looks like we're in for some sunshine. I'd like to thank everyone for a job well done. You've all worked hard on this cattle drive." He took his hat off and held it over his heart. "Therefore, I am proud to call you all cowboys. And Maggie, I am proud to call you a cowgirl."

They all tossed their hats. "Yee-haw!"

She laughed. What a great night.

David, one of the quieter boys, stepped forward. She knew what was planned because she'd been part of it.

"Joe, we have a petition here signed by all the members of Cowboy Quest. It says that we'd like to change our vote, and vote that Brandon doesn't get sent home."

Joe took the paper that she handed him. He glanced at Maggie, and she nodded slightly. He studied the petition. "I see that you all agree. Brandon, I'd like to hear what you think."

The boy stood. "I deserve to be sent home for all the trouble I caused. But I really want to stay. Cowboy Quest turned out to be pretty cool after all."

Joe grinned. "Then the majority rules. Brandon will not be sent home."

As she was leaving for her tent, Danny passed her. She gave her nephew an impromptu hug. "I'm very proud of you, Danny." Then she did the same for Brandon, who was walking with Danny. "Fabulous singing and playing tonight. I'm so proud of you."

"Thanks, Maggie," Brandon said. "And…uh… thanks for helping me."

The two boys headed for their tents.

Joe came over to her. "This was a wonderful night, and you did an excellent job. But everyone did something tonight except you, Maggie."

She shrugged. "Maybe my talent was putting the show together. It was fun, and I had a great time working with the kids and the cowboys."

"I could tell."

He took her hand, and she felt the familiar thrill run through her.

"Maybe a talent show would be just what we need at the end of every Cowboy Quest." He pushed his hat back with his thumb. "I think I'm going to make the talent show part of the program for sure. Care to stick around and run it twice a year?"

She laughed. "You never know. Someday I might take you up on your offer." He had to be joking. He knew she was headed back to New York just as soon as the program was over. That was where she made a living, what she knew, where she was raising Danny.

Yes, she'd be raising Danny. Even though there were the two incidents that Joe would have to report to Judge Cunningham, ultimately they'd had positive outcomes. Danny would most likely stay with her—and she was more than grateful.

She had Joe Watley to thank—for his program, for helping Danny and the other boys. For just being him.

Maggie knew she'd miss Joe desperately when she had to leave.

But there was no reason to tell him that she loved him. Nothing could be done about it. She didn't expect him to make such an admission either. He knew that she didn't belong here.

Still, in her heart she wished that Joe would tell her that he loved her. That maybe somehow, someway they could work out a compromise.

It wouldn't—couldn't—happen. So Maggie would just enjoy the week that she had left and make memories that would last her through whatever life held in store for her.

Chapter Sixteen

A week later, they all divided into four vans for dinner at the Mountain Springs Steakhouse for a last meal together.

It was a beautiful day, but Joe was in a gloomy mood. He didn't like when Cowboy Quest ended, because he'd miss the kids. This time he'd miss Danny and Maggie the most.

Maggie was at his side in the front seat. Danny, Brandon and Cody were in the back. The three had become real friends, and he was happy about that. He heard them exchange email addresses and phone numbers, and he gave Maggie's hand a clandestine squeeze when they talked about "working the

Cowboy Code." She squeezed his back and gave him a dazzling smile, yet he could see shadows under her eyes.

He wished he could take away her fears about Danny, but as long as Danny and she continued in a positive direction, they would be fine.

They drove slowly through the tiny village of Mountain Springs, which looked just like its name— a little oasis in the middle of two large mountain ranges.

"What an adorable town!" Maggie said. "It's so quaint. And look at that beautiful old theater! Please let me off here. I have to check it out."

He pulled over to the right. The theater was on the left. It looked historic with its saloonlike façade. The only way anyone would know it was a theater was by the huge, modern marquee on the front of the building.

"Be careful crossing, Maggie. With all those yellow taxis speeding up and down the street, I don't want you to get hit," he joked. There wasn't a vehicle coming for miles.

"Oh, no. Look." On the front of the grassy lawn leading up to the theater, someone was pounding in a For Sale sign.

"I hear that a developer from Aspen is looking to divide it into stores with apartments above where the practice rooms are," Joe said.

"What a shame to tear down this lovely old

theater," Maggie said. He could hear the pain in her voice.

"It is a shame, and it's breaking George Adams's heart to sell it to a developer, but he's moving to be closer to his daughter and grandchildren." He watched her closely for a moment.

"Maggie, we'll wait for you at the restaurant. It's only over there." He pointed to a rectangular one-story building with floor-to-ceiling windows and dark brown trim. "Take your time."

"Thanks." She got out and crossed in front of the van. When he looked back, she was talking to the person putting up the sign.

But he couldn't wait for Maggie at the restaurant. He didn't want to be away from her one more minute than necessary.

"Boys, go ahead and order without us. I'm going to the theater and wait for Maggie."

When he walked in, he found her sitting in the third row, watching a rehearsal of *Chicago*. A sign in the lobby stated that the performance ran every weekend during the month and was to benefit the local library.

It looked to him like the theater needed a benefit of its own.

He took a seat next to Maggie.

"Joe, do you know that Lillie Langtry, the Jersey Lily, played here? And look at these other names."

She held up a pamphlet. "Helen Hayes, Ethel and John Barrymore, Mary Martin."

She kept rattling off names. "It'd be a shame if it was made into condos or shops."

She tapped her feet and moved to the music, humming along with the chorus.

He could tell that she felt the music in every part of her body, and even in a whisper, she sang like a well-polished star. He could listen to her forever.

He'd wanted to ask Maggie and Danny to stay on his ranch indefinitely, but he couldn't do it. Nor could he ask her to marry him. He could see how she came alive in the theater. She'd never be happy on his ranch, in his life. She belonged in New York, on Broadway, not in this little town where the only theater they had was for sale.

She'd be leaving tomorrow, and he'd let her go. He had no choice—he knew it was for the best.

The piano suddenly stopped. "Maggie McIntyre?" A man with reading glasses perched on his nose and a clipboard in his hand hurried down the stage stairs to where they sat.

"It's really you. You're Maggie McIntyre!"

"I am," Maggie said with a smile. The man scooped up her hand and shook it warmly.

"Hi, Joe," he said, not taking his eyes off Maggie.

"George." Joe offered him his hand, but he

only had eyes for Maggie. "Maggie, this is George Adams. He owns this theater."

Maggie shook his hand. "Nice to meet you, George. I see that this beautiful landmark is up for sale."

He nodded. "The missus and I are moving to Utah. We want to be near our grandchildren." He turned to Joe. "Darlene had triplets."

"Yeah, I heard," Joe said. "Give Dar my best." They'd gone to school together, and Darlene had been Miss Rodeo Queen for all four years of high school.

"Miss McIntyre," George gushed, "it really is an honor to have you here. Would you like to stay and watch us rehearse? The cast would be honored."

"I'd love to, but I have a restaurant full of cowboys waiting for me to join them. I just stopped in to check out this beautiful theater."

"It is beautiful, isn't it? You don't see balconies like these much anymore. And all that marble in the lobby, it's as beautiful as the day it opened. We've taken good care of the old place since the '50s, but Darlene needs us."

"Well, I hope that whoever buys it doesn't change a thing and keeps it in just as good condition." Maggie stood, and the actors on the stage gave her a round of applause.

"Break a leg," she called.

As she left the theater with Joe, she stared at the For Sale sign, then shook her head sadly.

They joined the others at the steakhouse. Joe noticed that Maggie was unusually subdued during dinner.

He should fight for her, dammit. He *wanted* to fight for her. But he had nothing to offer her, only life on a ranch—a ranch that could never be enough to make her happy, and that wouldn't be the same when she was gone.

He had asked her to run the Cowboy Quest talent show twice a year, but she didn't even entertain the question. To ask her to marry him…he thought of Ellen and decided he didn't want to be hurt again.

After their last campfire together, Joe called for lights-out and disappeared into the bunkhouse with the rest of the cowboys. But in the wee hours of the morning, he appeared at her bedroom door.

"Maggie? Are you awake?"

She opened the door, greeted him with a sad smile.

"I'm not sleeping, Joe. Just thinking…"

I was thinking about how much I want you to ask me to stay.

"I just came to say goodbye to you."

Her heart sank.

"I wanted to say goodbye to you, too, but it's going to be hard," she said. "And I want to thank you. You've done so much for Danny and me—for all the kids."

She wanted to make love with him one last time, but he wasn't moving from the doorway.

"I'm going to miss you," she added.

"I'll miss you, too."

"I asked Ronnie to take us to the airport in the morning."

That startled him. "Why don't you want me to take you?"

"Because it's hard enough saying goodbye to you now."

He crossed the room to her bed. She moved over, and he sat on the edge, took her hand.

"Are you worried about Danny? Putting him back into the same situation?"

"He seems to have changed, but I won't know until I get back. I'm still a working parent, and that's not going to change."

"You told me before that you'd love teaching, and that you've taught kids before," Joe said.

She nodded. "But Danny is my first priority right now."

"Of course," Joe said. "You know, Maggie, Danny could come to the theater with you on occasion. He could do his homework there in a quiet spot instead of at home. Maybe he could even help you learn lines. And I've been thinking that Danny might want to tutor younger kids. That would give him a positive experience."

Joe was silent for several beats. Finally, he said, "I hope we can see each other again."

Her heart soared, and she could barely speak. This *wasn't* goodbye! It was an "I'll see you later."

She touched his cheek with her palm. "I hope we can see each other again, too."

Ask me to stay.

But Joe went silent again, and her heart took a nosedive.

He dropped her hand. "Maybe you could arrange to join us at the end of every Cowboy Quest, maybe put on another talent show. That was such a good experience for the kids."

"I thought of doing something like that in New York. That theater in Mountain Springs gave me an idea. Maybe I could buy an old theater, and…"

"In New York?"

He still wasn't asking her to stay—nor was he telling her that he loved her.

"Yes. A theater in New York," she answered.

Joe took a deep breath. "When will we see each other again?"

"Maybe I could visit you when I have time off, and you could visit me when you have time," she offered. "But if I'm in rehearsal for a new show I can't leave. I'd have to stay for the run of the show. And Danny has school, and…"

This was impossible. They were talking in circles. There must be a solution.

"I suppose we could do that," he said. "I'll be bringing my bulls to Madison Square Garden again for the Professional Bull Riders event in January."

"See? That's only about eight months away."

Who was she kidding—that was a lifetime away.

"I guess this is it then. See you later, Maggie."

She couldn't swallow, couldn't breathe.

"Goodbye, Joe."

He pulled her into his arms and kissed her gently, carefully, as if she'd break. Then he kissed her as if he couldn't get enough, slanting his mouth over hers, tongue sliding against tongue.

She hoped that he'd stay, make love to her one last time.

But he didn't. He tweaked his hat, and then he was gone.

And Maggie finally let her tears fall.

New York had lost some of its charm for Maggie. Instead of feeling the excitement in the air, she found herself thinking of the wide-open spaces of Wyoming. Every time she saw a horse on the street, she found herself thinking of Lady. She even found herself putting on her cowboy hat to go to the theater.

But above all, she missed Joe.

One day, in a melancholy mood, just for the heck of it, Maggie sat in the kitchen of her condo and called the real estate company in Mountain Springs that had the listing for the old theater.

"I'm sorry, it's sold," the agent said.

"Oh…um…thank you." She sighed, hanging up the phone, feeling deflated. She didn't know why hearing that it had sold devastated her so much.

She didn't know what had made her call, other than she'd been thinking about Cowboy Quest. If the theater could have a fundraiser for the library, why not have a benefit for Cowboy Quest? It would certainly help defray the costs for kids who couldn't afford clothes, or boots or hats, or traveling expenses. Or for Joe who might even need to buy more horses if the groups kept getting bigger.

She could have given dance lessons to local kids in those practice rooms upstairs, maybe even started a Cowboy Quest for kids who might be interested in theater arts, or a Cowgirl Quest just for girls.

But why was she thinking of Mountain Springs? She should be thinking of buying or renting places right here in New York.

She wanted to be near Joe, that's why.

But why was she even considering buying the old theater in Mountain Springs? She was in rehearsal now for a new musical. It had great songs, a Tony-winning choreographer and promising buzz.

Opening night was in a month.

Yes, things were going well.

Joe had sent a very complimentary report to Judge Cunningham, and Danny's charges would be dismissed if he stayed out of trouble for a year.

Danny had thrown himself into his schoolwork, had made some new friends in school and was ahead of his classmates, thanks to the Cowboy Quest teachers. He wasn't sneaking out, and they were talking more.

"What were you doing all morning, Danny?" Maggie asked as they sat down for lunch together.

"Emailing Brandon and the guys."

"How is everyone?"

"Great. Really great. Brandon's in a school play, and I've been emailing Joe, too."

Maggie tried to appear casual when she asked, "And how is Joe?"

"He's good. There's going to be another Cowboy Quest program in four months. They'll be moving the cattle from the summer pasture to the winter one."

Maggie flashed back to the cattle drive. It seemed so far away, yet it also seemed like yesterday.

"You miss Cowboy Quest, don't you?" Maggie asked.

"Yeah. And I miss my horse."

"I miss…everything, too." She was just about to tell him that she missed Joe.

Joe had called her a couple of days ago, and

they'd talked for over an hour. It wasn't enough, but she liked that fact that he'd finally told her that he missed her.

"Things just aren't the same here, Maggie. *I'm* not the same without you."

"I miss you, too, Joe. Maybe we can arrange to see each other again some time."

"You never know," he'd said.

She'd hung on to those three words. Was he planning a trip out here? Was he going to ask her to come for a visit?

Danny took a deep breath and looked at her.

"Something on your mind, Danny?"

He started to shake his head no, then changed his mind. "You know, Aunt Maggie, I wasn't very nice to you and Joe in the beginning. I thought you'd end up with him, and you wouldn't want me around."

He made a funny face. "The guys ragged on me something awful about you two."

"I know, and I'm sorry about that."

"But you didn't end up with him. How come?"

She sighed. "Joe has his life in Wyoming and I have my life here," she said, voicing what she'd been reminding herself for a week.

"But you could be in a show anywhere, couldn't you?" he asked.

"Yes, but New York has Broadway. That's the pinnacle of success."

"But you've already been on Broadway. You've reached the pinnacle."

He was right. She had attained her goal.

Maybe her agent could come up with an offer—something different—after her current contract ended.

But in a way, she had already received another offer. Joe had asked her to run the talent show at Cowboy Quest. But that wasn't really a job.

But it's the only thing I've been thinking about.

Joe had stuffed himself into a rented tuxedo and bought a dozen red roses from a street vendor. He wanted this to be a special night, a perfect night for all of them. The plan was to meet Dan at the theater for opening night.

He was risking his heart again on the chance that he could win Maggie over. He hadn't told Dan the real reason that he was coming to New York; he'd just said that he wanted to see Maggie perform, to be there on her opening night.

But the boy wasn't stupid. He'd probably already noticed that Joe was acting like a lovesick bull.

He couldn't wait to see Maggie again. And when she came onstage, she was mesmerizing. Joe didn't know much about musicals, but he did know that she had talent, lots of it. He wondered if she had to do her breathing exercises to calm her nerves.

He smiled, remembering how nervous she'd been during her first riding lesson.

But she'd learned quickly. During the cattle drive, she'd ridden like an old pro.

Look how happy she is, performing up there.

He wondered if he'd made the right decision in coming here, in making plans for them both.

As he listened to Maggie sing, he noticed the magical look on her face. He couldn't believe how gracefully she danced, how her melodic voice touched the audience.

His fears returned and laid heavily on his heart. He was thinking of himself, wasn't he? But if they just worked together, they could come up with a workable compromise, couldn't they?

Maggie looked in her dressing room mirror and saw Joe standing in the doorway with Danny, looking as handsome as ever. As delicious as he looked in a tux, she liked him better in jeans. She stood and rushed into his arms.

"I've missed you so much," she whispered into his ear.

"You were wonderful," he told her, handing her a bouquet of red roses.

"What brings you here?"

"My life hasn't been the same since you two left. New York is an exciting city. I think I could like it here."

Her heart was pounding fast in her chest. This was what she'd been wanting to hear. But the pieces just didn't fit.

She raised an eyebrow, suddenly skeptical. "Am I hearing you right?"

"I know nothing else but Wyoming, Maggie. Maybe my mother and father had the right idea—maybe I should experience more of the world."

"You've really given this a lot of thought."

"I have enough money to live on. I don't have to worry about that for a long time. And I plan on hanging out a lot with Dan, maybe doing some volunteer work for local organizations. Then I'll see you at the theater every night!"

"But Joe," Danny said, "what about Cowboy Quest? And what about the horses? And the cattle?"

"My ranch is in good hands with my crew and with my aunt. And I'll go back for Cowboy Quest."

"You don't belong here, Joe," Danny said, confused. "You have a ranch."

Tears stung Maggie's eyes. Danny was right. Even a thirteen-year-old boy knew that Joe would never be happy here.

But she could be happy in Wyoming—except Joe wasn't asking her to move to Wyoming.

"We'll talk more at dinner," Joe said.

Maggie grabbed her purse. "Let's go. I know a great place for Chinese food."

After walking to the restaurant and enjoying a great meal, Joe handed Maggie a folded pack of papers.

Puzzled, she opened the papers and scanned them. "I don't understand. This is the deed to the theater in Mountain Springs. But why? How?"

"It's yours if you want it. I was going to bribe you with it so you'd move to Wyoming for part of the year."

"Wait a minute!" She laughed. "You don't really want to move here, do you? Not if you've gone to all this trouble to buy a theater to convince me to move out there!"

"I was hoping that we could compromise—maybe we could split our time. And I have enough money, Maggie. We all could travel, see the world."

She grinned. "I think that's a definite possibility!"

"I know it's going to be hard for you to walk away from your career, Maggie, but take a chance on me."

"You're going to have to take a chance on me, too. Every now and then, I might miss New York and might miss Broadway—or maybe I'll decide in the future that I wouldn't want to return full-time. Just remember that I'm not Ellen."

"I realize that now."

Suddenly, Joe went down on one knee. "I love

you, Maggie McIntyre. Will you marry me? Life is just no good without you."

"Yee-haw!" Danny cheered. "Marry him, Aunt Maggie."

"Yes!" she yelled, pulling Joe to his feet.

Their mouths came together to seal the deal, and the patrons of the restaurant burst into applause.

Maggie looked into the eyes of the man she'd always love. "You didn't need to bribe me. I love you too, Joe."

Joe looked at Danny and Maggie and held up his glass in a toast. "To all of us."

"To all of us," Danny repeated, holding up a glass of milk.

"To my two cowboys," Maggie said, her heart overflowing with joy.

* * * * *

Look for the next book in
Christine Wenger's Gold Buckle Cowboys series,
HOW TO LASSO A COWBOY,
Coming soon,
wherever Silhouette Books are sold.

COMING NEXT MONTH

Available January 25, 2011

REQUEST YOUR FREE BOOKS!
2 FREE NOVELS PLUS 2 FREE GIFTS!

SPECIAL EDITION
Life, Love and Family!

HARLEQUIN®

A *Romance*

FOR EVERY MOOD™

Spotlight on
Classic

Quintessential, modern love stories
that are romance at its finest.

See the next page
to enjoy a sneak peek from
the Harlequin® Romance series.

*Harlequin Romance author Donna Alward is loved
for her gorgeous rancher heroes.*

*Meet Wyatt as he's confronted by both a precious
little pink bundle left on his doorstep and his neighbor Elli
who's going to show him the ropes....*

Introducing
PROUD RANCHER, PRECIOUS BUNDLE

THE SQUAWKING QUIETED as Elli picked the baby up, and
Wyatt turned around, trying hard to ignore the feelings of
inadequacy as Darcy immediately stopped fussing.

"Maybe she's uncomfortable. What do you think, sweet-
heart?" Elli turned her conversation to the baby.

"What do you think is wrong?" Wyatt asked, putting the
coffee pot back on the burner.

A strange look passed over Elli's face, one that looked
like guilt and panic. But it was gone quickly. "I couldn't
say," she replied.

"But you were so good with her this afternoon." Wyatt
put his hands on his hips.

"Lucky, that's all. I just...remembered a few things."
The same strange look flitted over her features once more.

Wyatt took the coffee to the table. "You fooled me. You
looked like you knew exactly what you were doing." So
much so that Wyatt had felt completely inept. A feeling he
despised. He was used to being the one in control.

Elli and Darcy walked the length of the kitchen and
back. After a few moments, she admitted, "I haven't really
cared for a baby before. The things I thought of were simply
things I'd heard about. Not from experience, Mr. Black."

Her chin jutted up, closing the subject but making him

want to ask the questions now pulsing through his mind. But then he remembered the old saying—*Don't look a gift horse in the mouth.* He'd benefit from whatever insight she had and be glad of it.

"I don't really know what babies need," he said. "I fed her, patted her back like you did, walked her to sleep, but every time I put her down…"

Wyatt almost groaned. Of course. He'd forgotten one important thing. He'd been so focused on getting the formula the right temperature that he'd forgotten to check her diaper. Not that he had any clue what to do there either.

Pulling calves and shoveling out stalls was far less intimidating than one tiny newborn.

"She's probably due for a diaper change, isn't she." He tried to sound nonchalant. This was a perfect opportunity. Elli must know how to change a diaper. He could simply watch her so he'd know better for the next time.

Instead, Elli came around the corner of the counter and placed Darcy back in his arms. "Here you go, Uncle Wyatt," she said lightly. "You get diaper duty. I'll fix the coffee. Cream and sugar?"

Oh boy, Wyatt thought, looking down into Darcy's pursed face, his smug plan blown to smithereens. He was in for it now.

Will sparks fly between Elli and Wyatt?

Find out in
PROUD RANCHER, PRECIOUS BUNDLE

Available February 2011 from Harlequin Romance